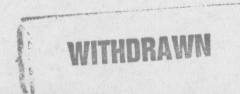

# Valentine to
# a Flying Mouse

# *Valentine to a Flying Mouse*

## LAURA HAWKINS

Houghton Mifflin Company
Boston 1993

*Library of Congress Cataloging-in-Publication Data*

Hawkins, Laura.
    Valentine to a flying mouse / by Laura Hawkins.
        p.   cm.
    Summary: During preparations for the fourth grade Valentine party,
Tammy meets the wheelchair-bound owner of the local bookstore who
helps her learn to cope with her parents' separation and to believe
in herself.
    ISBN 0-395-61628-X
    [1. Self-perception—Fiction.   2. Divorce—Fiction.   3. Schools—
Fiction.   4. Valentine's Day—Fiction.]   I. Title.
PZ7.H313517Val   1993            93-659
[Fic]—dc20                       CIP
                                 AC

Printed in the United States of America

BP   10   9   8   7   6   5   4   3   2   1

*Also by Laura Hawkins*

Figment, Your Dog, Speaking
The Cat That Could Spell Mississippi

*With love to Daryl —*
*who has always believed*

# *Valentine to a Flying Mouse*

# 1

"Guess what, Mrs. Crandall?" Tammy Collins said as her teacher swung into the classroom. "Someone stole all the valentines out of our valentine boxes."

"Let somebody else tell it, Collins," Eddie Wilcox grumbled. "You didn't have any valentines in your box for anybody to steal."

Tammy glowered at Eddie. "I did, too!" She *did* have valentines. One from Libby Grimes. One from Linda Cappanelli. And one from Jill Kramer. Tammy sighed. Three measly valentines. Not even enough to cover the bottom of her box. Not the most. Not the best. Not the biggest. And none of them yum tum and heart hum.

"Yum tum and heart hum" was something Tammy had made up to describe her father's hot chocolate. It wasn't the hot chocolate exactly, but the way it made Tammy feel when she drank it after coming inside on a cold, snowy day.

She felt the same way when her dad had told her that she was the most important person to him in the whole world. She and her sister, Meredith, he had said. That was before he left to live in another town, away from Tammy and her mom and Meredith. That's when Tammy discovered that her dad had lied to her. She wasn't the most important person to her dad at all. If she was so important, why hadn't he called her up on the phone or come visit, or at least sent her a valentine?

She wasn't important to him. She was only as important as she thought herself to be. Eddie Wilcox could gripe all he wanted, but Tammy was the first person to tell Mrs. Crandall about the stolen valentines. First was best and most important.

Mrs. Crandall eyed the fourth-grade class with disbelief. All twenty-five students were standing at attention at the back of the room, stationed at their valentine boxes, lids removed and tilted toward her so she could see the empty bottoms.

"Oh, surely not. Who would do such a thing?" Mrs. Crandall marched to the back of the room, inspecting each box. There were red ones and white ones, decorated with hearts and doilies and lumps of glitter and the names of the owners in big letters.

Since a week ago, when the boxes were finished,

handfuls of valentines had been brought to school by the students in preparation for the Valentine's Day party, two weeks away. They had been carefully inserted into the lid slits of the boxes of the owners to whom they were addressed. But now the boxes were all empty!

"It must have been a valentine monster that ate them," Marcella Starbuckle said. "He probably came in through one of the windows. Let's go outside and look for heart footprints. Then we can track him down."

"And get snatched away, too!" Jill wailed, on the brink of tears.

"Stop making things up, Marcella," Tammy snapped, making sure everybody heard the important way she had corrected Marcella. One thing Tammy possessed that no one else in the class did was a loud voice, which demanded everyone listen when she said something. But she would have gladly traded her megaphone voice for an oodle of valentines in her box. She would have traded anything to get back the "yum tum and heart hum" feeling that made her believe her father still loved her. Not believing made her a grouch; she didn't like being a grouch. Somehow, though, she couldn't help herself. "There's no such thing as a Valentine Monster," she grumbled at Marcella.

"Well, somebody took them," Libby reasoned. "They were here yesterday and now they're gone. Somebody sneaked in here after school yesterday or this morning when nobody was in the room and took them."

Tammy smirked at Libby. Libby was acting too much like a know-it-all. Tammy had to say something to prove that she was the best person in the class to figure out what happened to the valentines. "I bet I can find out what happened to them."

Even though everyone in the room had heard Tammy's boast, no one paid any attention to her.

"Libby's the one who can track down the thief," Linda said. "She's the best detective we have. She's smart and good at figuring things out."

Tammy stiffened. "Detectives don't always have to be the smartest. They have to be the best at asking questions. I'm good at asking questions."

"But you're not the best," Marcella said. "Libby's the best."

"Fine," Tammy said, rolling her eyes. "She can be the best at asking questions. I'll be the best at answering them."

"Does that mean you're going to solve the mystery of the stolen valentines?" Jill asked hopefully.

"Of course I am. But when I find out where they are, I might not bring them back. Why should I bring back a bunch of valentines that weren't sent to *me?*"

Linda quickly assured her, "Everybody in the class would give you a valentine if you brought back the stolen ones."

Tammy smirked. She didn't believe everybody would give her a valentine if she brought back the stolen valentines. But it might be enough if everybody agreed that she was the most important person in the whole class, if they gave her an award. Something that said she was a hero, that she could send to her father to prove how valuable she was.

"Does anyone know anything about this?" Mrs. Crandall asked.

No one said anything.

"Maybe we should all bring more valentines tomorrow and then set a trap for the thief," Ryan Soetart suggested. "My dad has a rat trap we could use."

Mrs. Crandall shook her head. "No rat traps, Ryan."

"Well, we could get our dads to camp out with us in the school overnight," said Billy Cameron. "I'll bring my baseball bat. Then POW! My dad can hit the thief right over the head. Knock the rat out cold."

Tammy wondered, would *her* father do something brave like that for *her*? The answer made her teary.

No. Her father lived miles away ever since Tammy's parents had separated. He would never come all that way for her.

"Mrs. Crandall," Eddie said, "My mom's not going to let me buy any more valentines to bring to school. When she finds out the ones I already brought were stolen, she's probably going to sue the school."

"There's no need for that, Eddie." Mrs. Crandall motioned everyone back to their seats. "And we're not going to buy any more valentines." She swayed thoughtfully to the front of the room. "We're going to hope that whoever took the valentines will return them." Then she smoothed out the front of her blue pantsuit. "But meanwhile, we're going to draw names. Just like we did at Christmas. And whoever's name you get, you will make one very special homemade valentine for that person. We're not going to let our party plans be spoiled."

Each person wrote his name on a piece of paper, folded it, put it in Mrs. Crandall's box, and then waited for a turn to draw a slip. Tammy drew Linda Cappanelli's name.

"Mrs. Crandall, Mrs. Crandall!" Marcella called, waving her arm like a flag. "Can I ask a real poet to help me write my valentine so it will be the best?"

Everyone groaned. "You don't know a real poet," Eddie scoffed.

"Yes, I do," Marcella argued.

"Not personally."

"I do, too. He owns a bookstore here in Riverview."

"Then how come nobody's ever heard of him?" Tammy asked skeptically.

Marcella shrugged. "I can't help it if you're a nobody."

Tammy gulped. She couldn't think of a single thing to say back to Marcella. Because, even though it was a joke, she was convinced that what Marcella had said was true. Tammy *was* a nobody. Why else would her father ignore her? Why else would she only receive three measly valentines?

Her eyes burned. But she couldn't let anybody know she was about to cry. Important people didn't cry. Important people didn't show their feelings. Her father was important. To her, anyway. He could make the best hot chocolate of anybody. But he didn't do that anymore. He didn't show her his feelings either. Not even a valentine. Important people didn't send valentines to nobodys.

# 2

The bookstore was the only one in Riverview, a tiny shop sandwiched between the hardware store and the beauty parlor. Maybe that's why the sign above its front window was designed to stand out so well, Tammy decided. It had to steal attention away from the other shops, just like Tammy wanted to steal Marcella's idea to persuade a real poet to help her write the best class valentine.

The sign was painted in curlycue gold letters against a background of red, reminding Tammy of an amusement park marquee. It looked flashy and daring and fun. "Papa's," Tammy pronounced. "Odd name for a bookstore," she said to herself. "Odd name for a poet." But it sounded warm and inviting and comfortable. She liked it.

Inside the store, the books weren't displayed on

shelves; they stood on low tables, rows of them zigzagging like a trail of upended dominoes waiting to be nudged.

Tammy might have tried pushing one of the books to see what would happen, but she heard a booming voice blasting out a gusty song in a language she didn't understand. Since she was the only person in the shop, and a little bell above the glass front door had tinkled when she entered, she was too afraid of getting caught to topple the books.

But nobody came to ask her why she was there! The voice kept right on singing!

Finally, she marched to the back of the store where the voice was coming from and yelled out, "Doesn't anybody know I'm here?"

The singing stopped. Then she heard a *tick, tick, tick*ing noise. It was the sound of the wheels on a wheelchair rolling over the hardwood floor.

"Welcome to Papa's!" the man in the wheelchair boomed at her. "You want storybooks? You want classics? Whatever you want, Papa's got."

Tammy stared. She hadn't seen very many people in wheelchairs before. None actually. She didn't know what to do or say. This person in the wheelchair was a poet? He didn't look like a poet, but then Tammy had never before seen a poet to know what one looked like either.

The expression on the man's thick face, the wide smile and dancing dark eyes, drew Tammy's attention away from the wheelchair. What could make the man so happy? Tammy wondered. Why wasn't he sad and angry because he couldn't walk?

"So. To what do I owe this pleasure?" the man asked.

"What pleasure?" Tammy still stared. She couldn't help it. She wanted to know what was wrong with the man that he couldn't walk on his own. She stared at his legs, as if they might tell her why they couldn't move.

She didn't see anything wrong with the man's legs. He wore a pair of pinstriped dress slacks and shiny black boots. He looked okay to her. Maybe he was riding around in the wheelchair for fun. He acted as if that might be the case when he let out a laugh that shook his whole body.

"The pleasure of you being here," he said. "Such a pretty young girl come into my store on a glorious snowy day."

"I'm not pretty," Tammy corrected him. "And it's not snowing outside. All the snow is on the ground. And it's dirty and slushy. Nothing pretty at all."

"You should look in the mirror some time," he said. "Such a halo of cherubic brown curls. Such an angelic face. Ah, but it is so sad. Such a shame to wear a frown on a face that so much wants to smile."

Tammy informed the man, "I can frown if I want to. Maybe I don't feel like smiling."

He nodded solemnly. "That is the sad part. That you don't feel like smiling. And because you don't feel like it, you don't see the pretty young girl that I do. You don't see flakes of milk falling outside either. You can't even imagine them. It takes a smile for make-believe to happen. But maybe I can help you believe in yourself. Even with a frown."

"I'm not here to believe in myself," Tammy scolded him.

"Don't tell me. Don't tell me," the man thundered, raising high a muscular arm, draped by a rolled-up white shirt sleeve, to his forehead in thought. He closed his eyes. "You want a great love story. For Valentine's Day. For your sweetheart."

Tammy blinked. Who did this man think he was? She was too young for a sweetheart. But he didn't seem to think that. Just the same, she told him so.

He spread his fingers so they covered his eyes, as

11

if he were concentrating on thinking hard. But then, when he peeked out at her between his fingers, he winked as if he knew more than she did about what she wanted.

Tammy couldn't help herself. She laughed at how comical the man looked. "No, silly. I'm looking for the poet."

He threw his arms up so violently that Tammy thought he was trying to do a backward flip in the wheelchair. Now *there* would be a trick that Tammy would like to see.

"Of course! How could I not place you? You have cultivated literary tastes. You read poetry. You probably even write poetry."

Tammy shook her head.

The man shrugged. "It is not too late to start. Never too late." He heaved his arms at the wheels of his chair so they would turn, leading her to a table toward the front. "Come. Come. Follow Papa. Papa will find just the book for you. Papa's got Keats. Shelley. A little Yeats. A little Browning. Aha! Yes. Here we go." He snatched off a volume from the table. "Walt Whitman," he said. He opened the book to the exact page he wanted, as if he knew by heart where a particular passage was and read, "I am larger, better than I thought. I did not know I held so much goodness."

12

"I didn't come here for a book," Tammy interrupted. "I came to talk to the poet. Are you the poet?"

She hoped he wasn't. He acted stranger than how she had imagined a poet might act. He clowned around too much. Poets were supposed to act serious. Otherwise, who would ever believe what they wrote? And poets were not supposed to be in wheelchairs.

A gurgling, echoing laugh filled the store. "Am I the poet?" He spun his chair around so fast to face her that Tammy blinked in wonder of how he had done it so quickly. "Well, let's see. I do write poetry. Although none of my poems have ever appeared in a book."

Tammy made a face. "That stupid Marcella Starbuckle! I should have known better than to listen to her!" She stomped off towards the door.

"Wait! Wait! Come back!"

Tammy reluctantly shuffled back to the man. "This has all been a mistake," she explained. "Somebody told me that a poet owned this bookstore. I thought she meant a poet with poems published in a book. Obviously, she was wrong. I have to go now."

"No, no, no, no, no. Tell me why you need a published poet."

Tammy shrugged. She supposed it wouldn't do any harm to tell the man why she needed a published poet. "To write a valentine for me, of course. If he were good enough . . . like those people who wrote those books," she said, pointing to the volumes on the table next to them, "to write a poem for my special valentine at school that'll be the best." Because of the puzzled look on his face, she added, "A special poem written to my valentine by a real poet would make me the giver of the best valentine in my whole class."

"Hmmm," the man said in a low voice, thinking.

"But since you aren't a real poet . . ." Although she didn't say it, since his poems hadn't been good enough to publish in a book, she had changed her mind about asking him to help her. "Maybe I'll just forget the whole thing."

The man threw out his hands again. "Not only do you not believe in yourself, but you don't believe in anybody else either. Such a sad, sad way to be."

"Then how come you don't have your own book?" Tammy asked, pointing again to the table. She had already made up her mind. She had decided that she definitely didn't want this man to write a poem to her valentine. He might say stuff in the poem about snowflakes made out of milk and talk about angel faces. Tammy didn't want imaginary stuff in her poem. She wanted something real.

"Maybe someday I will have my own book," he said. "Then I might be famous twice."

That got Tammy's attention. "How were you famous the first time?" she asked.

He smiled. "I am Papadakis. The only survivor of an airplane crash that killed two hundred people. That's how I'm famous."

"Wow," Tammy said, edging closer. "Is that why you're in a wheelchair?"

Papadakis nodded thoughtfully. But then he jerked, thumping his arms on his chair. "And who are you?"

"I'm Tammy Collins. A nobody. I've never even been on an airplane. What kind of a name is Papadakis? Papadakis," she repeated his name thoughtfully. "Is that all there is? Don't you have a first name?"

"With a name like Papadakis, who needs a first name?" he asked, laughing. "*I* certainly don't. So if Papadakis is name enough for me then it is who I am. Papadakis, the poet. And if I say that I am a poet, then I am. Being sure of it myself is all that is necessary."

Tammy reconsidered. Since he seemed so sure of

himself, maybe Papadakis was good enough to write her poem after all. His name was unusual enough to make him sound like a real poet.

"So you'll do it? You'll write my valentine for me?" she asked.

Papadakis shook his head.

"Why not?" Tammy said.

"For me to write your valentine would be like you using my wheelchair to walk. It would get you around, but what would be the point? It would be silly for you to ride when you can walk."

"But I can't write a good valentine," she wailed.

Papadakis's bushy dark brows jumped up and hid beneath the hair that spilled over his forehead. "Not if you say you can't, no. Not if you don't believe in yourself." He winked. "Not if you don't believe that things that don't usually happen can happen."

"I wouldn't know where to start," Tammy explained.

"Start by loving yourself," Papadakis said.

Tammy frowned. "That's stupid — to love yourself. Everybody wants other people to love them. What's loving yourself got to do with anything?"

Papadakis rubbed at his whisker-stubbled chin

thoughtfully. "Everything. How can you love any-body else . . . write a good love poem . . . if you don't know anything about loving yourself first?" He paused so she could think about it for a moment. "I won't write your poem for you. But I *will* teach you how to love yourself so you can write it."

"Nobody can do that," Tammy said. "If I don't like me, how can you make me change my mind?"

Papadakis shrugged. "There has to be something you like about yourself."

Tammy nodded. "I like my voice. It's very distinct. Like somebody talking through a megaphone. Maybe I'll be a cheerleader some day. Maybe when I grow up I'll get a job as a circus announcer."

Papadakis grinned. "See what I mean? When you start thinking of things you like about yourself, then you can imagine all kinds of things."

Tammy started to smile, but then she thought of something — a reason why what Papadakis had just said might not be true. "Do you like being in a wheelchair?" she asked him.

Papadakis grew quiet. "No. No, I don't."

"Are you ever going to walk again?" Tammy asked gently.

Papadakis shook his head thoughtfully. "I will never again feel the crunch of snow beneath my feet . . . never ride a bicycle or kick off my shoes."

"And I'll never be able to write a poem," Tammy said.

Papadakis picked up a book from the table, marked a certain page with a bookmark he pulled from the side of his wheelchair, and handed the book to her. "Read this," he said, "and think about some other good things about you, like your circus announcer voice, when you read it. Bring the book and your thoughts back tomorrow."

Tammy accepted the book, but she wasn't sure she would bring it back the next day. She was afraid there weren't any more good things about herself to bring back with the book, and that made her feel depressed — just like when Papadakis admitted that he would never walk again.

# 3

A strange feeling hovered over Tammy when she walked out of Papadakis's bookstore. At first she thought it might be because the interior of the shop seemed like a whole different world to her — it was warm and friendly. Outside was cold and lonely. Stepping out of one and into the other made her feel dizzy.

But then she thought it might be the book in her hand. She was confused about that book. When she accepted it from Papadakis, she had planned to throw it away in the nearest trash can. Now that she looked at the title, *Greatest Love Poems of All Time,* she thought she might be able to find a poem for her valentine in it that she could copy and claim she had written. But then she remembered the expectant look on Papadakis's face. She decided she might try writing a poem of her own by taking one and changing some of the words around.

She considered opening the book to take a look at the poems, but someone was watching her. Down the street, a shadowy figure had hopped back into a store doorway when Tammy stepped out onto the sidewalk. Well, two could play this game, she decided. She walked away slowly, and at the most convenient doorway hopped into it, disappearing from view. Then she peeked around the corner to see who had been following her.

Ha! It was Libby Grimes. What was Libby up to? Why was she following Tammy? Was she trying to steal Marcella's idea to ask Papadakis to write her valentine too? No, Tammy reasoned, Libby never asked anybody for help with her homework. She must be working on the case of the stolen school valentines.

Well, Libby was in for a surprise, Tammy thought to herself, chuckling. Libby would never find out who stole the school valentines. Because Tammy was not going to tell her, and she was the only one who knew!

Still, she worried when she saw Libby glance up and down the street, and then disappear inside the bookstore. If Papadakis wouldn't write a poem for Tammy, he wouldn't write one for Libby either. Or would he? Tammy used to think her dad would never leave her, but he did. If she couldn't trust her dad, why should she trust Papadakis?

She felt her eyes sting and her throat tighten up. She knew that if she let them, tears would stream down her face. She *had* to think about something else, but she couldn't find a single good thing.

She quickly swung out of her hiding spot and ran down the street toward Kreske's Variety Store. She would look at the items in the window, she decided — that would relieve her worries that Papadakis might be, at that very moment, writing a poem for Libby.

She looked at the display of red satin heart-shaped boxes of candy in the window. It always made her feel better to look at hearts and cupids and roses. Sometimes she would go into the store and pretend to pick out a special valentine for her dad. She would slip the valentine under her coat and walk out without paying for it. She told herself that if she were ever caught stealing, she wouldn't tell the people in the store how to call her mother. She would give them her father's name instead, so he would *have* to come back to Riverview to see her. But nobody had ever caught her. She wished somebody would. Actually, she wished she could catch herself before she did it. But she didn't know how.

Jill stepped out of Kreske's, smiling so big her braces showed, hugging a bag containing her purchases. But when she saw Tammy, she closed her mouth.

"Hey, Jill, what did you buy?" Tammy asked.

"Oh, nothing," Jill said, stepping around Tammy, suddenly in a hurry.

"Something for your valentine?" Tammy guessed. "Mrs. Crandall said not to buy anything."

Jill flinched, then tried to pass Tammy. But Tammy jumped back in front of her, standing squarely in Jill's path. She was afraid Jill had bought the best valentine in Kreske's for her school valentine, and Tammy wouldn't have a chance to give the best one, no matter what she did.

"It's a secret," Jill said.

Tammy couldn't help herself. "Guess I'm going to have to tell Mrs. Crandall that you bought your valentine," she threatened.

"You wouldn't," Jill said meekly.

Tammy nodded that she would.

Jill sagged. "It's just that I wanted to make the best valentine of all. And I didn't have the paper I needed at home. My valentine is going to be so terrific! I'm making the biggest valentine ever! It's going to be huge!"

"Who's it for?" Tammy asked, hoping Jill had

drawn her name and she would be the one who would receive the biggest valentine.

"We're not supposed to tell," Jill answered.

"We're not supposed to buy anything either," Tammy taunted her.

"Oh, all right," Jill said, giving up. "I drew Marcella Starbuckle's name."

"That liar!"

"I can't help whose name I drew," Jill defended herself.

Tammy smirked, which was the expression she did best. "No, but you don't have to make her such a big valentine."

"That's going to be the fun part," Jill confided. "Making the valentine. It's going to be three feet tall. Nothing less would fit Marcella. You know, because of the wild stories she always tells."

Tammy didn't care that Jill's valentine would "fit" Marcella. In fact, she hoped Marcella would get just what she deserved for making up that story about Papadakis being a real poet. "Can't I just peek in your bag?" Tammy asked, hoping to get a glimpse at Jill's valentine materials, still wishing they were meant for her.

Jill hesitated. But then her enthusiasm got the better of her. She handed the bag over to Tammy. As Tammy reached for it, it slipped out of her hands, toppling over. Its contents of sheets and sheets of pink paper spilled onto the ground, covering a puddle between them. The brown water blotted the centers of each piece as they fell into the puddle, swallowing them up, one by one.

"Oh, no! Look what you did!" Jill danced around the puddle, wringing her hands, watching her precious paper sink. "You did that on purpose!"

"It was an accident," Tammy said in a weak voice, a voice nothing like her usual loud one.

"I'm going to tell on you, Tammy!"

Tammy's face burned at being accused of ruining Jill's paper on purpose. The only thing she could think to do was to lash out at Jill. "No you're not. Because then you'd have to tell you were doing something wrong yourself."

"You big bully!" Jill barked at Tammy. "You were jealous of me giving Marcella the biggest valentine in the class, so you ruined it!"

"Me? Jealous of Marcella Starbuckle?" Tammy laughed. But it was a hollow laugh. There was some truth to what Jill said, but she had to keep from admitting it. "How could I be jealous when *my* valentine is going to be the best one in the class?"

Jill didn't say anything. She ran away. Tammy

wanted to call her back and tell her she was sorry, but the words wouldn't come out of her mouth. What was wrong with her? Why was she always doing things that made people run away? Like her father, for instance. Maybe Papadakis was right — maybe she needed to figure out how to love herself before she drove everybody else away.

All the way home she tried to think of a poem about herself. First she read one of the poems from the book Papadakis had given her. It was a poem written by somebody named Elizabeth Barrett Browning. It was very dramatic, listing all the ways the poet loved somebody.

Tammy tried to imitate the poem. She tried to think of things she liked about herself as she made up the poem, but just like she had told Papadakis, she didn't have any good qualities.

How do I love thee? Let me count the ways.

I love your hair,
you grizzly bear

I love your nose,
a wilted rose

I love your mouth,
Has it gone south?

I love your smile,
a junkyard pile

I love your ears,
crocodile tears

To tell the truth,
I'm a goof.

By that time, she was home. She didn't feel any
better about herself, but she *did* feel good that she
had actually composed a poem! Her good feeling
didn't last long, though. When she checked the
mailbox before going into her house, there were no
valentines in it for her. Absolutely nothing in the
mail from her father.

# 4

Tammy heard a terrible racket upstairs when she walked into her house. Somebody was pounding with a hammer. By the sound of it, Marcella Starbuckle would have thought that a monster was up there. But Tammy knew it was only her sister, Meredith, working on her latest science project.

Meredith was in seventh grade, but everybody always said she acted older than that. When Tammy asked her mom why Meredith acted like such a know-it-all one time, her mom said that ever since Tammy's dad left, Meredith had started acting more "mature."

If by "mature" her mother meant weird, Tammy reasoned that only the return of her father could save the Collins household. That's when she figured out that Meredith was the reason her father had left in the first place.

No wonder he didn't want to live with them

anymore. He didn't want to hear the *blam, blam, blam* of a hammer when he came home from work in the evening. He didn't want to smell the putrid odor of some chemical coming from some experiment Meredith was cooking up. He might even have been afraid that Meredith might try to make a monster!

Tammy had told all of these things to Meredith, dozens of times. Especially when she was angry, she told Meredith that she was the reason their father went away.

Meredith would roll her distant blue eyes at Tammy and say, "Grow up." Then she would act high and mighty and go back to whatever experiment she was working on, never letting on that she'd even heard Tammy.

But Tammy knew that Meredith *did* hear her, because sometimes, after a terrible fight between them, muffled whimperings filtered through Meredith's closed bedroom door. Then Tammy would feel bad. She knew Meredith wanted their father back as much as Tammy did. When Meredith cried, Tammy sensed that she had given up hope that their dad would ever return, and then Tammy would cry, too. But she never told Meredith she wasn't sure her sister was the reason their dad left. Tammy didn't know the reason, and that scared her as much as his having left. Ever since he'd done so, she was scared of any kind of change in her life. That's why now, as she slumped on the living room sofa, a tiny peep made her jump.

What was that? *Peep, peep, peep.* There it was again! Tammy looked all around the living room. And then she spotted it. A small metal cage with wood shavings in the bottom of it. And swinging inside the cage was ... *eek!* A white mouse.

Tammy loved animals. She loved her cocker spaniel, Buttons. It suddenly occurred to her that loving animals was a good thing about her. People who loved animals were sensitive and kind and caring, weren't they? It was something she could tell Papadakis that was good about her! She jumped up from the sofa and ran to the cage that sat on an end table near the easy chair across the room.

The mouse was cute. He was a white ball of fluff. With itty-bitty red eyes. And itty-bitty pink ears, and an even ittier-bittier pale pink nose. He stopped swinging when Tammy came near the cage. He looked straight at her and wiggled his three-inch pink tail, which was just as long as his body. Tammy thought that was unusual for the mouse to wiggle its tail. Dogs wiggled their tails, and lambs and goats. But a mouse?

"Hey there fella," Tammy cooed at the mouse. "What's the matter? Are you glad to see me?"

Tammy unhooked the little fastener on the cage door and opened the miniature gate. The mouse darted through the opening and right into Tammy's hand!

Tammy laughed. The mouse skittered across her palm and then crawled around to the top of her hand. Then he tickled his way up the length of her arm to her neck!

This mouse could climb!

"Itty-Bitty! Itty-Bitty! Stop tickling me or I'll die laughing," Tammy sputtered.

Itty-Bitty stopped all right. He fell from her neck, down the front of her blouse and *plop!* into her pocket. He lay wedged in the pocket with the tip of his tail and end of his tiny nose barely peeking out.

Tammy laughed and laughed at the sight of him. Carefully, she touched one finger to his tiny head and stroked him. "You are a very daring mouse, Itty-Bitty. And funny, too. I think I like you."

She knew she should put Itty-Bitty back in his cage. She knew that he probably belonged to Meredith and that her sister would come looking for him soon, when she was ready to begin her science project. But Tammy didn't want to give him up. He was so adorable and charming. And best of all, he made her laugh.

"I'm hungry, Itty-Bitty. How about you? Want to go find something to eat?"

Hmmm. There was a problem. What did a mouse eat, she wondered. Cheese, of course.

But there was no cheese in the refrigerator. Her mother had used it all the night before to make macaroni. Well, maybe Itty-Bitty could eat what she ate, until she found out what it was that mice like to eat other than cheese.

From the refrigerator, she pulled out two slices of bread, the peanut butter and a box of raisins. Maybe mice liked ant sandwiches, she speculated. Ant sandwiches were what her father used to fix her for lunch to take to school. That was a whole year ago, but it seemed like ages and ages.

Tammy had been eating ant sandwiches for lunch and after school ever since he left. It seemed to be the only link she had with her dad. And she always wondered, when she slathered the peanut butter onto the bread and sprinkled on the raisin ants, if he were still eating ant sandwiches where he lived, too.

She broke off a tiny bit of bread and offered it to Itty-Bitty in her pocket. The mouse nuzzled the big crumb, rolling it around and around where he held it between his two front paws. And then he ate it!

She took the sandwich, the book Papadakis had loaned her, and Itty-Bitty in her pocket up the stairs to her room. There she flopped down on her bed and fed Itty-Bitty some peanut butter from her sandwich. She even gave him one whole raisin of his own to eat.

She opened the book and thumbed through the pages, glancing from poem to poem, looking for something that might look familiar. She found a poem by a person named Robert Burns that said love was "like a red red rose, that's newly sprung in June."

That gave Tammy an idea for a valentine to Itty-Bitty. She took out a sheet of paper and wrote:

Roses are red
Violets are blue
You're better than flowers
Since you spring in February, too.

She laughed hysterically at the funny valentine. Especially when Itty-Bitty "sprung" out of her pocket, scampered across her bed and disappeared over the edge.

Tammy jumped up to go find him. But she couldn't continue the search because Meredith knocked on her bedroom door.

"Oh, it's you," Tammy said, after opening the door. "I can't be disturbed right now. I'm writing poetry."

"Tammy!" Meredith pushed past her into the room. "You took my mouse! He isn't in his cage downstairs."

"What mouse?" Tammy asked innocently.

"You know what mouse," Meredith snapped.

"You brought a mouse into this house? Hey! That rhymes," Tammy said, lighting up. But then she rolled her eyes at her sister, the same way Meredith always did to her.

"Where is he?" Meredith said, dashing around Tammy's room, bending down on the floor to look around.

"What would you do with a mouse?" Tammy asked innocently.

"He's part of my science project," Meredith explained. "I'm going to teach him how to run through a maze. Record how quickly he learns. Now where is he?"

"That's stupid," Tammy said. "Who cares whether a mouse can run through a maze?"

Meredith rolled her eyes. "I wouldn't expect somebody like you to understand. Now where's the mouse!"

Tammy shrugged.

Meredith's face flushed with anger. "Okay, you little thief, I'll just wait till Mom gets home and then you'll really get it."

Tammy smirked. "You're the one who'll get it when Mom finds out you have a mouse loose in the house."

Meredith reconsidered. "Oh, just forget it! I'll get a new mouse."

"Wish I could get a new sister," Tammy said.

"Nobody would want to be your sister," Meredith said. "Including me. You're a thief!"

Tammy scowled at Meredith. "Well, you're a . . . a . . . a Frankenstein. Nobody wants to be around you. Not even a mouse. You're the reason Dad left."

Meredith closed her eyes loftily and jiggled her head, her most famous expression. "You little dope. Dad didn't leave because of me. He left because of you!"

Tammy's eyes widened. "Me! Why me?"

Meredith strolled to the door. "Who wants to be the father of a thief?"

She disappeared into the hall. Tammy slumped down on her bed. Could it be true? Could her father have left them because he thought Tammy was a thief?

Itty-Bitty wiggled across the bed. Tammy cupped her hands and closed them around the mouse, lifting him to her pocket, inserting him there.

"You like me, don't you, Itty-Bitty?"

Itty-Bitty bounced up and down in her pocket, peeping at her. His mousely antics made Tammy laugh. But it wasn't the same carefree laugh as before.

She found a box in her closet that she had used to store toys in. She dumped them out. But what would she use to make a nice, soft bed for Itty-Bitty?

She didn't have wood shavings or newspaper or anything like that. If she went looking for some, Meredith would get suspicious. So she opened the bottom drawer of her dresser, pulled it out and carried it to the box, dumping its contents. All of the school valentines fluttered out of the drawer and into the box.

Tammy hesitated a moment. She felt sorry that she had taken the school valentines, even if they would make a perfect bed for Itty-Bitty. In fact, now that she had Itty-Bitty to love and him to love her, she had intended to take the valentines back to school somehow. She didn't need them anymore. But no one at school loved Tammy the way Itty-Bitty did, so he deserved to have the valentines for his bed.

"There you go, Itty-Bitty," Tammy told him. "Bet no mouse ever had a bed of valentines before. See how much you're loved? I'm going to take real good care of you."

Itty-Bitty liked the bed. He scampered all over it, wiggling his nose at it, smelling it. Then he began chewing on one edge of an envelope. Tammy thought that would keep him busy for a while. She would go see if she could find some lettuce for him to eat.

"There you are, Tammy," her mother said, greeting her in the kitchen. "Good day at school?"

Tammy shrugged. "It was all right. Are you still going to bring treats to our class Valentine Party?"

"Of course, I am," Mrs. Collins said. "I'm getting off work especially to be there."

"Mom," Tammy began. "How come we never hear from Dad?"

Mrs. Collins unloaded a stalk of celery and a carton of eggs from her grocery bag. She acted like she didn't want to answer.

"Oh, I suppose he's probably busy," she said between trips to the refrigerator.

"What's he busy at?"

"Well, he's found a job in Rossville. Selling medical supplies."

Tammy wondered, "Can't he sell medical supplies here in Riverview?"

Mrs. Collins shrugged. "Oh, I suppose he could."

"But he doesn't want to. Right? Because he doesn't want to live here anymore."

"I suppose that's it," she said.

"So he's never coming back. Right?" Tammy hoped her mother would argue with her. But she didn't.

"I've told you before, Tammy, that your father's going away has nothing to do with us. He wasn't happy here. He needed time to be away to figure out why he wasn't happy."

Tammy could tell that her mother didn't want to talk about her father anymore. But she was sure she knew why he didn't want to live in Riverview with them — because of weird Meredith and the fact that her mother worked too many hours as a nurse at the hospital.

She swallowed thickly. And it was just possible that he didn't want to live with a thief.

# 5

"I think I'm in love," Linda Cappanelli whispered to Tammy at school the next day.

"Why would you think that?" Tammy asked.

"Because somebody gave me a valentine," Linda said.

Tammy looked puzzled. "It's not even Valentine's Day yet."

"I know," Linda said. "So the person who gave it to me must like me a whole lot. Right? Because he gave it to me so early."

He? A boy gave Linda a valentine? Tammy looked around the classroom. Ryan Soetart? Eddie Wilcox? Billy Cameron? Who was the stupid boy who gave Linda a valentine so early! Now Tammy's valentine to Linda would mean nothing. She could never top a valentine given to Linda by a boy.

"Who gave it to you?" Tammy asked, hoping to

make whoever it was feel sorry he had done such a stupid thing.

But Linda wouldn't tell. She smiled, and her eyes glanced down.

"Want to come over to my house after school?" Tammy asked Linda.

Linda shook her head. "I can't. I have basketball practice."

Tammy rolled her eyes. She couldn't understand why Linda wanted to play basketball. She was the the only girl in their fourth-grade class who played basketball. And Linda didn't even play on a girls' team! She practiced with the sixth-grade boys. Aha! Tammy suddenly understood that Linda's valentine probably came from a sixth-grade boy. Maybe Linda wasn't so dumb for playing basketball after all. She wanted to know exactly how Linda had managed to get a boy to give her a valentine.

"You could come over to my house after basketball practice," Tammy urged. "I won't be home until then anyway. I have to go somewhere."

"All right," Linda agreed.

Tammy was happy that Linda would be coming to her house; maybe then she would find out all about the valentine from the boy. But she wasn't happy that Libby had overheard her tell Linda about going somewhere herself after school. Everybody in class seemed to have forgotten about the stolen class valentines — everybody but Libby Grimes!

That made Tammy nervous. She was sorry now that she took the valentines, even though Itty-Bitty liked them a whole lot to chew on and burrow around in. She wished she could bring them back to school and put them back the way they were, but she couldn't now that Itty-Bitty had used them for a bed. Maybe everyone would forget that they were missing . . . if only she could make Libby stop trying to figure out who took them.

At recess, when Libby was on the swings, Tammy grabbed the swing next to her. "I saw you downtown yesterday," she said to Libby.

"You did?"

Tammy nodded. "And I know what you were doing."

"I was looking around," Libby said.

"You were following me," Tammy confronted her.

Libby didn't say anything, but Tammy could tell by the look on her face that she was right.

"If you know what's good for you, you'll stop playing detective," Tammy threatened.

"Sure, I'll stop," Libby assured her. "Because now I know how to find out all I need to know."

Tammy's face fell. Libby knew she took the school valentines! How did she know? Tammy hadn't said one word to Papadakis about it.

"What are you going to do about it?" Tammy asked in a gruff tone of voice.

"You'll find out sooner or later," Libby teased her.

Tammy jumped out of her swing so abruptly that it wobbled side to side and bumped Libby. "You think you're so smart, Libby Grimes," she yelled with her megaphone voice. Then she stomped off, sticking her thumbs in her ears and waving her fingers at Marcella Starbuckle, who had bounced over to the swing set to take her place in the swing. "Liar!" she accused Marcella as she passed her.

Tammy walked back inside the school, but she quickly ducked out of sight when she saw Jill talking to Mrs. Crandall in the hall. She was afraid that Jill might be telling their teacher how Tammy had ruined her paper the day before, and that Jill might not explain that it was an accident.

She watched them talk seriously for a few minutes. Then Mrs. Crandall nodded her head and Jill followed her to the main supply room. Then

41

Tammy saw Mrs. Crandall bring out a long piece of white paper that had been used as a banner to announce parents' night. She gave the piece of paper to Jill.

That wasn't fair! Jill should have to get her own paper, Tammy thought. But she couldn't say anything about it; not after she suspected that Jill might have told Mrs. Crandall on her.

"Ah, Tammy, you're just the person I've been wanting to talk to," Mrs. Crandall said, noticing Tammy lurking in the hall. Tammy wanted to dash back outside, but now she was caught. That tattletale Jill!

"Hi, Mrs. Crandall," Tammy said in her sweetest voice. "Have any erasers you want me to dust?"

Mrs. Crandall smiled. "No, Tammy. You did such a good job dusting the erasers after school the other day that they won't need it for a long while."

Tammy beamed.

"But there's something I want to ask you about." Mrs. Crandall started walking back to their classroom. Tammy walked cautiously alongside her. "Did you see anybody enter or leave the classroom the other day when you dusted the erasers for me? I didn't think about your being around that day after school until now. I thought maybe you might have noticed someone. Someone who might have taken our class valentines."

Tammy didn't say anything for a moment. Her mouth wouldn't move, and her tongue seemed to be stuck to the roof of her mouth.

Finally, she shook her head. It wasn't a lie. She hadn't seen anyone. But then she panicked. If she didn't say she saw someone, Mrs. Crandall might get suspicious and figure out that Tammy was the one who stole the class valentines!

"Wel-l, now that you mention it, Mrs. Crandall," Tammy began. "I did see a few people."

"Yes? Who?"

"Well, I saw Libby Grimes in the hall. And Jill Kramer was there, too. Oh, and I saw Marcella Starbuckle outside. She was talking to herself."

"Hmm," Mrs. Crandall murmured. "Well, that could be a lead of some kind, Tammy." She sighed. "I just wish that whoever took the valentines would bring them back. I've been getting a lot of phone calls from parents who have been upset by this whole thing. I tell them that I'm sure whoever took the valentines will think twice about it and return them. After all, why would anyone want valentines that belong to someone else?"

Tammy nodded, thoughtfully, sympathizing

with Mrs. Crandall. "I suppose whoever took them really must like valentines," she offered.

"Or maybe whoever took the valentines hated for anyone else to have them," Mrs. Crandall speculated.

"Could be," Tammy said with as mature a voice as Meredith's. "Maybe it's possible whoever took them didn't want to be embarrassed by not getting very many valentines."

Mrs. Crandall nodded. "I just wish that person could know how much joy the valentines would have brought to other people. I bet that person doesn't know that those valentines would have meant twice as much to the ones they were sent to than to the person who took them. And I bet the person who took them doesn't know that love is always greater given than received."

Tammy smiled sweetly at Mrs. Crandall. "You have a real way with words, Mrs. Crandall. I'm starting to notice words more now than I used to," she explained. "I'm reading and writing poetry."

"Good for you, Tammy," Mrs. Crandall said. She smiled, squeezing Tammy's arm with approval.

For a moment, Tammy thought she might muster enough courage to tell Mrs. Crandall that she had taken the class valentines, but somehow she just couldn't. She couldn't say something that would make Mrs. Crandall disapprove of her — not when she had just impressed her by telling about the poetry.

"Mrs. Crandall?"

"Yes, Tammy."

"I don't think anybody but a few parents really cares if the valentines are returned. Everybody is having fun making one special valentine. Nobody even misses the other valentines."

"Maybe so," Mrs. Crandall said. "But I bet whoever took them would feel a whole lot better bringing them back. Everyone in class would feel better, too. Knowing what happened to them."

Tammy nodded. "I guess it's sort of like my dad moving away," Tammy said. "Losing him was bad. But not knowing why he left was worse."

Mrs. Crandall studied Tammy with awe. "You are developing a real way with words yourself, Tammy."

Tammy beamed. She felt good about Mrs. Crandall's compliment. There *was* something that made people take notice of the particular words she chose, when she used words in just the right way.

But what was she going to do about everybody

else's words — the stolen valentines? Mrs. Crandall was right; she didn't feel good about those words at all.

# 6

"Has anybody come around asking nosy questions about me?" Tammy asked Papadakis the first thing when she went to the bookstore after school.

Papadakis rubbed at his thick chin. Then he nodded. "Somebody was asking. It is wonderful to have somebody care about you like that. Yes?"

"No," Tammy said. "It was that snoopy Libby Grimes. I bet she wanted to know why I was here, right? She wanted to know if I told you anything about valentines, right?"

Papadakis nodded.

"But you didn't tell her anything? Because you don't know anything about any school valentines? Do you?"

"No. I don't know anything about any school valentines. You want to tell me?"

Tammy shook her head. She wasn't about to let Papadakis know that she was a thief. Instead, she told him about Itty-Bitty. Except for the part about stealing him from Meredith. "So I need a book about mice," she told him at the end, "so I can take good care of Itty-Bitty."

Papadakis wheeled himself right to the book that told everything there was to know about mice. He handed it to her after he placed it in a paper bag and took her money. Then he smiled. "It is a very good quality to love animals. You must have read the poem from the book I loaned you. Did you think of any other reasons to love yourself?"

Tammy shrugged, not wanting to admit that although she had written two poems and used some very "mature" words when talking to Mrs. Crandall, there were still more bad things about her than good. She showed Papadakis the poem she had written about herself. "I told you before that there's nothing good about me," she explained. "Otherwise, my father wouldn't have gone away."

Papadakis read the poem silently and waited a few moments to say something, as if he were choosing his words very carefully. "Sometimes, Tammy," he said thoughtfully, "bad things happen to good people. Like your father leaving you. Like when the airplane I was in crashed. You didn't do anything to make your father leave, and I didn't do anything to cause the airplane to crash. Both things just happened."

Tammy wailed in her megaphone voice, "But it isn't fair! I want my father back. Don't you want to walk again? More than anything?"

"More than anything," Papadakis admitted.

"Have you tried? Really tried?" Tammy asked.

"Have *you*?" Papadakis questioned her. "Have you asked your father why he left? Or if he will ever come back?"

No, she hadn't called her father or written him any letters. She was afraid he would say, like Meredith had told her, that he wasn't coming back because Tammy was a thief.

"No," Tammy mumbled. "How about you? Have you ever tried to walk without your wheelchair?" Tammy challenged him again.

"Once," Papadakis admitted.

"What happened?"

"I fell flat on my face," Papadakis said, smacking his palms together to indicate how suddenly and violently he had collapsed on the floor.

"Then all that talk yesterday about how a person had to believe in himself was something you made up," Tammy accused him. "You don't believe in yourself enough to try walking again. Why should

I believe in myself to write poetry? Or talk to my dad? Or anything? You're just a fake. Nothing you say is true."

Papadakis's eyes widened with alarm. After a few moments, he pleaded, "Some believing is easier than others. The doctors said I could never walk again. I believed them."

"Why should you believe *them*?" Tammy said louder, angry with Papadakis for not being something she thought he was. "Here's your stupid book back," she said, shoving the volume of *Greatest Love Poems of All Time* into his hands and turning on her heels to leave. "You aren't a real poet," she said, as she marched to the door. "A real poet would believe things can change. A real poet would believe in make-believe."

She hoped that Papadakis would call her back, that he would try to explain more about why he hadn't at least tried to learn to walk again. But he didn't. She felt her throat dry up and her eyes sting and her stomach ache. It was just like the way she had felt when her father left. She had felt weak and achy and helpless.

The little bell tinkled above the shop door as a customer walked in. Tammy started to walk out of the door as the man stepped in, but she saw Libby Grimes through the front window, heading toward the book shop. Instead of passing through the open door that the man held for her, she ducked back into the shop to hide from Libby. She would stay and find out what Libby had come to see Papadakis about. By spying on them, she'd find out what progress Libby had made in searching for the school valentine thief. And she would see if Papadakis had been telling her the truth about Libby. She wasn't sure she trusted him anymore.

The bell tinkled above the door a second time and Libby stepped into the store. Tammy crouched low behind a book table so Libby wouldn't see her. She waited for Papadakis to help the customer select a book, and when the man left, she crept closer to where Libby and Papadakis talked.

"I'm back," Libby greeted Papadakis. "Remember? You said if I came back some time you might be able to help me."

The usual happy sound in Papadakis's voice was gone, but he tried to act glad to see Libby. "Ah, yes. Liddy."

"Libby. Libby Grimes. The one who was in here yesterday asking you about Tammy Collins."

"Something about valentines," Papadakis said.

Tammy froze where she crouched at the corner of the table nearest Papadakis.

"You said you might know more about Tammy

after you talked to her today. Did you talk to her today?"

There was a moment of silence. "Oh, yes, I talked to her. Or maybe I should say that she talked to me. She made me think about something I hadn't thought about in a long time. She has started me thinking, all right. About myself."

"Any clues for me?" Libby asked. "About what I should do about Tammy?"

"Hmm," Papadakis murmured thoughtfully. "Yes. Yes, I have a suggestion. Invite Tammy's father to come to school."

"I already thought of that," Libby said. "My mother called him up on the phone for me. But he said he couldn't come."

Papadakis didn't say anything for the longest time. And when he did, Tammy didn't hear him, because she crept away from the two of them, towards the door. She couldn't listen to any more.

When another customer entered the shop, Tammy dashed out the open door, blinking back tears. She was right that if she ever got into serious trouble, her father would never come and rescue her. But how could Papadakis be such a traitor? How could he help Libby catch Tammy and prove that she was the school valentine thief?

# 7

"Where've you been?" Linda Cappanelli asked Tammy. Linda was sitting on Tammy's porch swing holding her gray cat, Mississippi, stroking his fluffy fur. "I've been done with basketball practice and home to change. I brought Mississippi with me. It's okay, isn't it?"

No, it was *not* okay. Tammy wondered if cats could smell mice. Would Mississippi smell Itty-Bitty in her room and try to hunt him?

"Can he stay out here?" Tammy asked, hoping Linda wouldn't take Mississippi up to her room.

Linda shook her head. "I'm afraid of losing him."

Reluctantly, Tammy showed Linda and Mississippi into her house and led them up the stairs to her room. She hadn't even had a chance to make sure Itty-Bitty was safe and sound in the closet, in his box full of school valentines!

"Did you bring it?" Tammy whispered secretively to Linda.

"Bring what?" Linda asked.

"The valentine you got from a boy."

"Oh. That." Linda's dark eyes glanced down with modesty. Then she sheepishly nodded her head. She pulled an envelope out of her coat pocket and handed it to Tammy.

Tammy took the envelope and sat down on her bed next to Linda, who held Mississippi in her lap. She didn't want to seem eager to look at the valentine. Because then it would appear that she was excited that her friend had gotten something she didn't get. But already, as Tammy slowly pulled the envelope flap open, she was getting that itchy angry feeling she always got whenever she envied somebody else.

"It's not a very big valentine," she said, pulling the card out. "If somebody really likes somebody else, they get the biggest card possible."

"No they don't," Linda argued. "Size doesn't have anything to do with it."

"Yeah, well, it doesn't have lace or satin or glittery letters on it."

"Boys don't like that kind of stuff," Linda argued. "They like simple valentines like this." She pointed to the picture of a big red heart on the front

54

of the card. "They like hearts that say 'Be Mine.'"
Which the one on the front of the card said.

Tammy opened the card. There was a verse on
the inside. It read: "Because of you, I'm a better
person." Then under that was written in pencil,
"And a better basketball player. Your friend, Cory
Richards."

Tammy wilted with relief. "This card doesn't
even say anything about love! Gee, now I know
why. Cory Richards! He's not even very cute.
There's a lot better-looking boys in sixth grade
than Cory Richards!"

Linda's face lengthened. "I think he's cute," she
defended Cory. "And I'm glad he didn't choose a
card with a whole bunch of mushy stuff all over it.
I don't like those kinds of cards."

Tammy closed her eyes and made her mouth
pinch. Sure, Linda didn't like mushy stuff. But she
would have liked it if Cory Richards had said some
of it on his card. She would have liked a card that
had "love" written on it somewhere.

"Well, it's still a valentine from a boy," Linda
argued. "Know any other girls in our class who got
a special valentine? From a boy?"

Tammy had to shake her head. She was impressed with the valentine, even though she wasn't
about to show any sign of it to Linda. Inside, she

longed for someone to give her a card just as special.

"Are you going to give him one back?" she asked Linda.

Linda nodded. "But I don't know whether to make one or buy one. I looked at the valentines in the stores and none of them seem to fit. Have any ideas?"

"Why don't you make one?" Tammy suggested. "It's more personal." She said that to make the valentine that Cory had given to Linda seem not so special, since he had bought it from a store.

"Say something like, 'Roses are red, violets are blue, since you gave me a valentine, I'm giving you one, too.'"

"I can't say that!"

"Why not?"

"Because then it would sound like I was just giving him a valentine because he gave one to me."

"Well?" Tammy shrugged her shoulders. "That's why you'd be giving him one, wouldn't it?"

"No. I like him, too. I have to say something about liking him."

"You mean mushy stuff?"

"No. Not mushy stuff. Just 'I like you.'"

"Okay. How about 'Roses are red, violets are blue, even though you're ugly, I like you.'"

Linda stood up from Tammy's bed, brushing Mississippi aside. "Cory's not ugly! He looks nice. Gee, Tammy, you don't know anything about writing valentines!"

Tammy stuck out her chin. "I was just trying to help. You said you wanted ideas."

Linda sat back down on the bed. "Ideas yes. But I don't want insults!" She picked up the poem that Tammy had written about herself. "What's this?"

Tammy quickly snatched the poem from Linda's hand. "Oh, nothing."

Linda shrugged and pulled Mississippi to her and stroked him on her lap so that the gray cat's back rose in rhythm to her touch. The cat yawned and stretched and then hopped down onto the floor, sniffing at the carpet. "Well, what's with all that 'roses are red and violets are blue' stuff? I don't like that part. It sounds corny."

Tammy stood up, worried about Mississippi, who strolled to her closet door. She couldn't let him smell Itty-Bitty! "That's how homemade valentines always start," she said to Linda, following the cat to the closet. "They always start with flowers."

"Well, I don't like it," Linda said. "I've never liked valentines that start out that way."

Tammy scowled. She had planned to start out her valentine to Linda that way. She liked the roses and violets part. If Linda didn't like it, that was too bad. Tammy was still going to give her a valentine with the roses and violets in it. And she was going to prove to Linda that talking about roses and violets in a valentine at first was the proper way to write it!

"But listen to this," she enticed Linda. "Roses are red, violets are blue, you play great basketball, and I like you, too."

Linda smiled. "I like that one. Let me write it down before I forget it." She borrowed a piece of paper and a pen from Tammy's desk and started writing. "This doesn't mean I'm going to use this for sure," she explained. "I might think of something better myself. It's just an idea. I still might take out the part about the flowers."

Tammy shrugged. "I don't know what you've got against flowers."

Linda looked up from her writing. "I just think there ought to be something better. That's all."

Tammy sniffed. "Hmm. Your cat is acting funny," she said, watching Mississippi run his nose along the bottom edge of her closet door. "Maybe he needs to go out."

"You just don't like cats," Linda said, finishing her writing.

"I hate snoopy cats," Tammy said.

"Mississippi isn't snoopy." But Linda stopped what else she was going to say because Mississippi was now running his paw along the bottom of the closet door, as if he wanted to find a way to open it. Linda asked, "Have you got something in there a cat might like? He usually doesn't act like this."

"He needs to go out," Tammy repeated. No sooner had she said it than Mississippi nudged open the closet door and disappeared like a flash inside. "Oh, no! Get him out of my closet! Get him out of my closet!"

Linda sprang off the bed to retrieve Mississippi. But Tammy blocked her entrance to the closet. She couldn't let Linda see Itty-Bitty's bed of school valentines, could she?

Tammy quickly pounced on Mississippi and flung him out of the closet. He landed with a thump in the center of the room, crying out from the surprise of having been tossed.

"Tammy, that was a mean thing to do!" Linda shouted. "Come on, Mississippi, we're going home." She snatched up the cat, cast a disgusted look at Tammy and marched out of the room, tromping down the stairs.

Tammy didn't follow Linda. She stayed to find out what had happened to Itty-Bitty. She searched through every last school valentine, thinking Itty-

Bitty might have burrowed himself down under them to get away from the cat. But she couldn't find him anywhere.

She sat back on her heels and moaned. Why was it that everything she did turned out to be such a mess? It all started when she stole those school valentines, which seemed like a good idea at the time but had caused her so much trouble with Libby Grimes and Papadakis and now Linda.

Besides that, those valentines caused her to lose Itty-Bitty. But even if she hadn't stolen the valentines, she had stolen Itty-Bitty from Meredith. Stealing was ruining her life more than it was already ruined by her dad moving away.

She made herself a promise: No more stealing. If only she could find Itty-Bitty again.

# 8

Four days passed with no sign of Itty-Bitty. Tammy searched high and low for the white mouse. Every day, she yanked out the box of school valentines from her closet to the center of her room and rummaged through them frantically. He wasn't there, even when she overturned the box and scattered the pile of cards!

At first, Tammy cried. If she lost Itty-Bitty for good, she thought she would die. After all, she had already lost her father. Wasn't that enough? And it occurred to her that she loved Itty-Bitty as much as her father; in fact, losing Itty-Bitty made her realize just how much she loved the mouse. She had given up on believing that her father would ever come back or at least try to talk with her and visit. But she wouldn't give up on Itty-Bitty. She wouldn't!

She tossed out every pair of shoes she owned

from her closet floor. Each time she searched, she yelped with fear. What if Itty-Bitty had been in one of those shoes? What if he had gotten out of her room and run down the stairs and out the door when someone opened it? What if her dog, Buttons, had eaten him? What if he had chewed a hole in a far corner of her closet wall and was running around inside the walls of the house?

The possibilities of what happened to him were endless, just as the reasons for Tammy's father having left could be any of a number of things. But Tammy knew that Itty-Bitty couldn't survive without food and water, so she continued to fill a small bowl with lettuce and cheese and cereal and another with water and place them in the closet. It was her way of showing him love. And every morning when she woke up, the first thing she said to herself was that she believed Itty-Bitty would come back. She *had* to keep believing that. She had to!

She thought about Itty-Bitty being lost as she put out the food and water. She also thought about her father. He was lost to her, too. In putting out food and water and still believing Itty-Bitty would come back, she realized she had never done anything similar for her father — like sending him a valentine herself or calling him up on the phone or simply believing that he still loved her. It occurred to her that her father might need some sign of her love as much as Itty-Bitty needed the food and water. Why hadn't she thought about her father this way before?

On the next Monday, it happened. After school, Tammy once again took everything out of her closet to search for Itty-Bitty. She took all of her shoes out, searching the depths of each shoe. All the while, she said to herself over and over, "I *will* find Itty-Bitty. I will!" But he was not there. Then she glanced up from where she had been examining her shoes — something small and white was scaling the front leg of her floor-to-ceiling shelf across the room. It was Itty-Bitty!

Tammy sat very still so as not to frighten the mouse away. Now how did he get out of the closet? How, for that matter, had he gotten out of the deep box that held his bed of valentines? She would probably never know the answer to that question. But she was convinced it was because she had *believed* Itty-Bitty would come back that he did. And now she believed that Itty-Bitty could do anything. He had survived four days on his own, hadn't he?

Once atop the shelf, Itty-Bitty skittered back and forth on the top ledge. "Itty-Bitty!" Tammy called out to him, surprised and overjoyed to have found him. She was about to jump up and go retrieve him from the ledge when Itty-Bitty flew off his perch, gliding the ten foot span with his legs spread-eagled and his tail propelling him. He *flew* to Tammy, landing on the bed beside her!

Tammy didn't move. She couldn't believe what she just saw. Did she actually see it? Itty-Bitty jumped, didn't he, she asked herself. But if Itty-Bitty had jumped from the shelf ledge, he would have landed far short of the bed, she estimated.

No. He had flown. He had actually flown from the shelf ledge to the bed, landing only an arm's length from her! Then he shimmied to the corner of the bed, hopped onto her outstretched hand and tickled the length of her arm with his tiny feet, dropping from her neck into her pocket.

"Oh, Itty-Bitty!" Tammy exclaimed. "You are no ordinary mouse. You can fly!"

Itty-Bitty peeped at her, rolling around in her pocket so he lay tummy-up, looking very pleased with himself.

"Were you flying to me?" she asked him. "Did you do that just for me?"

Itty-Bitty peeped.

Tammy laughed. Itty-Bitty had done it! He had actually flown off the shelf. She eased Itty-Bitty out of her pocket, holding him gently in her hand. She stroked him on his back. Then she walked the length of her room to a curio shelf that hung in the far corner. She set him carefully down on the shelf among a collection of glass unicorns.

Tammy walked back to her bed. "You can do it, Itty-Bitty," she said to him. "You can fly."

She watched Itty-Bitty carefully. Again, he tottered precariously at the shelf's edge, as if he were building up some inner fortitude. Then it happened. He sailed through the air, legs extended, tail twirling with a rotary motion. Only this time, he hovered over the bed a few seconds and dropped with more precision, near the corner of the bed where Tammy had crouched.

Itty-Bitty scampered to her again, scaling her arm to her neck, free-falling into her pocket.

Tammy sat there for a few moments. She didn't know what to do. She didn't know whether to yell out with joy or run and tell someone, or crawl into her bed and pull the covers over her head because Itty-Bitty's flying was too wonderful!

Instead, she took Itty-Bitty out of her pocket again and stroked him in her hand. "You can fly, Itty-Bitty. You can fly," she told him. She was sure that he was listening to every word she said. And she was sure that he was happy that she believed in him. In fact, she suspected that her believing in Itty-Bitty was part of what helped him to fly!

Itty-Bitty peeped and rolled over so she was able to rub his tummy. She couldn't help thinking that she was not the reason that Itty-Bitty could fly — she wasn't good at inspiring animals or people to do things. She wasn't good at doing anything. Something else must have made Itty-Bitty fly. Did Meredith do something to Itty-Bitty that made him fly? Did she feed him some chemical? Tammy decided to find out.

She carried Itty-Bitty to her closet again. This time she curled him into the pocket of one of her blouses that hung inside. "I'll be back in a minute, Itty-Bitty," she told him. Itty-Bitty wiggled his whiskers, then washed his face with his front paws.

A putrid chemical wafted out of Meredith's room. What was that Einstein doing now? Tammy knocked. She was feeling so good about Itty-Bitty's ability to fly that she felt courteous.

"Go away, I'm busy," Meredith mumbled.

Tammy pushed through the door anyway.

"Didn't you hear what I was saying?" Meredith grumbled to Tammy.

"What are you doing?" Tammy began.

"Important work on my science project," Meredith muttered, not looking up from her work table.

"Something really stinks in here," Tammy said.

"It's the polymer."

"The what-a-mer?"

"The plastic polymer I'm using to make my worm maze."

Tammy stepped closer to see what her sister was doing this time. "You're making another maze? How come you like mazes so much?"

"I'm interested in animal and invertebrate behavior."

Tammy wanted to tell Meredith to try experimenting on herself, since she was such an animal. But she didn't; instead she smiled. Wouldn't Meredith be surprised to know that *she* had a flying mouse! Tammy was dying to tell her. But she knew she couldn't — not when she'd stolen Itty-Bitty from Meredith.

Tammy leaned over Meredith's shoulder and watched her sister pour a clear liquid goop into a round plaster mold.

"Why are you making a worm maze?" Tammy asked. "I thought you were going to get another mouse."

Meredith stopped pouring, setting the pan of

liquid back on its rack atop a bunsen burner. "Mr. Dorset couldn't get me another mouse in time for the science fair." Mr. Dorset was Meredith's science teacher. "So I'm going to use planarian worms. I can find plenty of those in any freshwater stream."

Tammy nodded, acting supportive of Meredith, when all she really wanted to know was anything Meredith knew about Itty-Bitty. Was he a special mouse? Had he been taught to fly? Was he fed an overdose of some kind of chemical in a laboratory and that was what made him fly?

She didn't want to hear about planarian worms. "Where does Mr. Dorset get things like mice?" she asked.

Meredith shrugged. "Oh, he buys them from some supply company that sells experimental animals to science labs."

Tammy nodded thoughtfully. "But how can a person know if the animal hasn't been fed something radioactive?"

Meredith eyed Tammy critically. "Why would anybody want to do that? The animal would die. And nobody would buy animals from a place like that again."

"So they don't do anything to the animals? They don't give them anything special? Like extra helium? Or extra oxygen? Or pills that might make them do stuff they wouldn't ordinarily do?"

Again, Meredith eyed Tammy with a quizzical look. "No, silly. That would wreck any experiments anybody might want to use the animals for."

Tammy straightened up and said with a huff, "Well, I think it's just horrible that anybody would use animals for experiments in the first place!"

Meredith stood up from her chair and pulled on her jacket. "Hmm," she said suspiciously. "I didn't know you were such an advocate of animals' rights. How about worms? You like them, too? I'll bring you back some from my trip to the river."

"I hate worms," Tammy said, wrinkling her nose.

"That's right," Meredith said, smiling. "You never could bait your own hook when we used to go fishing. Dad always had to do it for you."

"I never used to want to go fishing in the first place," Tammy whined. "Dad only went because it was what you wanted to do. If you had let *him* pick something he wanted to do, he probably never would have left."

"He liked fishing," Meredith argued.

"Not as much as you."

"Well, I remember a few times we went to the

dumb old amusement park because *you* wanted to go. We could never get you off 'The Flyer' to go home. Dad hated that ride. But you made him go on that roller coaster with you."

"He liked it!" Tammy screamed.

"Yeah, well, how many roller coasters you suppose he's ridden on since he's been gone?"

Tammy's lower lip drooped. She only wished she knew. "How many times you suppose he's gone fishing?" she said, attempting to argue.

Meredith shrugged.

"One thing's for sure," Tammy said slowly, thoughtfully. "I haven't been on any roller coasters since Dad left."

"I haven't gone fishing," Meredith admitted. Then she stomped out of her room to begin her hunt for planarian worms.

Tammy was left feeling bad about liking roller coasters, when only a few minutes ago she had felt wonderful about Itty-Bitty flying. Darn that Meredith! She had made her stop believing in herself. No, Tammy admitted silently — no one could make her stop believing in herself — only Tammy could do that.

She stomped down the stairs to find her mother. Mrs. Collins was in the kitchen, fixing stir-fry for supper. The gingery smell of the stir-fry reminded

Tammy of her dad, because he always liked stir-fry. "Hey, Mom, think we could go to the amusement park this weekend?"

Mrs. Collins glanced up from her cutting board and stopped chopping vegetables for a moment. "Tammy, the amusement park doesn't open until April. You're two months too early."

Tammy sighed. "Mom, what would you do if Buttons started doing something really weird?"

Buttons, Tammy's cocker spaniel, looked up from underneath the kitchen table. Tammy loved Buttons. She and her dad had gone together to pick Buttons out of a litter of puppies. When her dad first left, Tammy was certain he would come back again. He wouldn't leave Buttons, would he?

"Is there something wrong with Buttons?" Mrs. Collins asked.

Tammy shook her head. "I'm just supposing."

"Well, while you're supposing, why don't you set the table?"

Tammy pulled out three plates from the cupboard and placed them around the kitchen table. The table had room for four, chairs for four and placemats for four. Did she have to be reminded again that her dad was missing? She tried picturing four plates on the table. She closed her eyes and tried to remember what it was like a year ago when her dad was still living with them. But it was difficult to picture it. She opened her eyes. It was too hard for her to believe now that her family would ever be together again. She ran upstairs to her room.

There she retrieved Itty-Bitty from the pocket of her blouse in the closet. She set him on the bed, stroking him so his eyes looked like little red-hot candies when she tugged at his head. Just touching him and looking at him and knowing what she knew about him — he could fly! — made her feel a whole lot better.

# 9

Tammy woke up the next morning with the most terrific idea she had ever had in her life! It was an idea that would solve three problems at once. It was brilliant!

First, she was dying to tell somebody about Itty-Bitty. She couldn't tell Meredith. Meredith would be angry Tammy had stolen her mouse. And she couldn't tell her mother because she was afraid she would be ordered to get rid of Itty-Bitty.

But she *could* tell Linda. And by telling Linda, she would explain her odd behavior of throwing Mississippi out of the closet a week ago. Which would make them friends again. That was the second great thing about her idea.

The third great thing was that she had figured out a way to keep Itty-Bitty and his flying a secret. She would convince Linda to help her form a secret club. It would be called The Fantastics. And the membership requirement would be that every member had to have something "fantastic" to share with the other club members, something everybody would know about but had to keep secret.

The fourth wonderful thing about Tammy's plan was that she knew Libby would want to join. Libby's detective nature would make her want to know everybody's secret. And if Libby joined, then Tammy could get Libby to help her figure out why Itty-Bitty could fly. Libby would forget all about the stolen school valentines and concentrate on Itty-Bitty.

At school she singled out Linda, who was hanging around the water fountain before class. "Sorry about treating Mississippi the way I did," she greeted Linda. "But I had a reason."

"Yeah," Linda agreed with her. "You are mean and you hate animals."

"That's not true," Tammy argued. "In fact, I was trying to save an animal's life when I tossed Mississippi out of my closet. I have a pet mouse. I was afraid Mississippi would catch my mouse and eat him!"

Linda looked relieved. "Well why didn't you say so?"

Tammy shrugged. She had to think of something other than the fact that if she had let Linda help get Mississippi out of her closet, Linda would have discovered she was the school valentine thief.

"I didn't want anybody to know about my mouse," Tammy confessed. Which was true. "He is not an ordinary mouse. But I can't let anybody know that. Not unless they swear to keep it a secret."

"What's so special about him?" Linda asked.

"I can't tell," Tammy whispered. "Unless you want to join my secret club. It's a club called the Fantastics. That's because everybody in the club has something to share that is 'fantastic' about themselves. And something that has to be kept secret."

"I don't have anything like that," Linda said.

"Of course you do," Tammy reminded her. "You have a valentine from a sixth-grade boy."

"You didn't tell anybody, did you?" Linda gasped.

Tammy shook her head. "And I won't. If you'll be in my club."

Linda shrugged. "All right. But I can't meet right after school."

"I know," Tammy said, rolling her eyes. "Basketball practice. We'll meet after that at my house."

Linda nodded. "But who else is in the club?"

"Wel-l. We could ask Libby," Tammy schemed. "As long as there's something fantastic about her."

"Of course there is. She's friends with rich old Mr. Spencer. She got him to donate his carousel to the city."

"But that isn't a secret anymore. Everybody knows about that."

"Yes, but nobody but Libby knows what the inside of his house looks like."

True, Tammy thought. And she decided she'd like to know what the inside of Mr. Spencer's house looked like. Who wouldn't want to know all about a mansion! Knowing that secret would be good enough to make Libby fantastic.

"Okay, that's good enough."

"Well, what about Jill? If we had four members, we could call ourselves the Fantastic Four."

Fantastic Four. Now why didn't Tammy think of that? She felt a little disappointed that she hadn't thought of that name before Linda.

"What's fantastic about Jill?" Tammy asked.

"I know something!"

"What?"

"I can't tell. Only Jill could tell. But it's fantastic enough to be in our club."

Tammy wiggled her clenched lips. "Jill may not want to be in our club. She's mad at me."

"I'll ask her," Linda suggested. "We meet at your house after basketball practice. Right?"

"Right." Then Tammy said carefully, "But you won't bring Mississippi, will you?"

"Not this time," Linda said, smiling at Tammy. "Even though he is a fantastic cat."

Tammy smiled back.

# 10

After school, Tammy ran to "Papa's" bookstore. She wanted to know if Papadakis had any books that said anything about flying mice. Itty-Bitty's flying made her forget all about being upset with Papadakis; her anger magically disappeared. "My mouse can fly," she blurted out to him first thing.

Papadakis smiled. Then he recited some poetry she didn't understand. "O spirit of love! how quick and fresh art thou...even in a minute: so full of shapes of fancy, that it alone is high fantastical."

"What does that mean?" Tammy asked him. "Do you believe me about my mouse flying or not?"

"It was written by Shakespeare. William Shakespeare. It means that love can work many wonders. And of course, I believe you! I am Papadakis, the only survivor out of two hundred. I of all people will believe the incredible."

Tammy was quiet a moment. Then she asked, "Are you saying that love is what's making Itty-Bitty fly?"

"What else could it be?"

Tammy shrugged. "Well, at first I thought maybe somebody had done something to Itty-Bitty at the supply place where he came from. You know, fed him some chemicals to make him do stuff like flying. But my sister, Meredith, said that wasn't true."

Papadakis shrugged. "What else then but love?"

Tammy gulped. "I think it's because I believe Itty-Bitty can do it. I believe in him."

"Believing in something or someone is the same thing as love." Papadakis smiled. "My guess is that your mouse wants to fly. But that special ingredient . . . love from you . . . makes the difference as to whether he wants to do something and can actually do it. You help him do it by loving him *and* believing in him."

"Itty-Bitty is so easy to love," Tammy said thoughtfully.

Papadakis's dark eyes twinkled. "I have something fantastic to show you myself. But I'm not quite ready yet. In a few days maybe."

"Tell me! Tell me!" Tammy begged, not wanting to wait. "I'm starting to love surprises," she explained.

"You are full of surprises yourself," Papadakis said. "I have never seen you smile so much. Maybe you are almost ready to write that poem for your valentine, huh?"

"Maybe I am," Tammy said confidently. "I'll keep trying," she assured him before she dashed out of the store in her haste to get home for the Fantastic Four club meeting, forgetting to ask him if he had any books about flying mice. No, she thought, as she beamed from within, she was sure that Itty-Bitty was the only known flying mouse in the world. There would be nothing in books about him.

She had just enough time to get home and hide the stolen school valentines before Linda and the others showed up for the meeting. She stuffed them into the far corner of her closet — no one would ever look there.

She couldn't wait for the meeting to start. She even made some punch and brought a tray of cookies to her room, just for the occasion. Still, she was a little nervous as to whether Libby and Jill would come. And if they did, how would they act towards her?

They did come! At five o'clock, Linda, Libby, and Jill knocked on the front door. Tammy smiled widely when she showed them in. Libby acted like nothing had happened between them. Well, it had been Libby who spied on Tammy in the first place!

But Jill fidgeted all the way up the stairs to Tammy's room and wouldn't look Tammy in the eye. She hadn't forgotten that Tammy had ruined Jill's paper, accident or not.

Tammy served the cookies and punch first. She didn't want anyone to be hungry when she put on the show she had planned in which Itty-Bitty would fly. After the refreshments, she said, taking charge, "Let's get down to business." Then she cleared her throat and said that they would take turns telling what is fantastic about themselves. Then everybody would be joined.

"But what if something isn't fantastic enough?" Jill asked, worried.

"I know. After each person tells, the other three get to vote if it's fantastic enough for the person to be joined."

"But what if it isn't?" Jill asked.

"Then you have a chance to come up with something else at the next meeting," Tammy said. "Is that agreed?"

The others nodded.

"Jill, you go first."

"Why do I have to go first?"

"Because your name comes first in the alphabet," Tammy reasoned.

Nobody said anything. But that was because Linda and Libby were still eating cookies. Jill didn't eat any cookies at all, on account that they'd get stuck in her braces.

"Okay," Jill finally said. "The thing that is fantastic about me is that I can whistle 'Row, Row, Row Your Boat' through my braces so it sounds sort of like a harmonica."

"You can?" Tammy asked with surprise. "I never knew that. Do it so we can hear."

Jill's face reddened. But she sat up on her heels and faced the others, who sat cross-legged on the floor. She whistle-hummed "Row, Row, Row Your Boat."

Everybody clapped at the end.

"Okay, Libby, it's your turn," Tammy commanded.

Libby's eyes shifted. She heaved a deep breath. "This is something I've never told anyone. And if anybody here tells it, I will say you are lying."

No one doubted that she would.

"When I was in the Spencer mansion at Christmas, I found this lever in the parlor that makes a bookshelf open. Behind the bookshelf is a secret compartment."

"No!" Tammy exclaimed.

Libby nodded her head, eyes wide. "Is that good enough?"

"I think it's good enough," Jill said.

"Me, too," Linda agreed.

"Okay, Linda," Tammy said, wanting to hurry the meeting along so she could show Itty-Bitty.

Linda pulled out the valentine from Cory Richards. She passed it around the circle. Tammy didn't look at it much because she had already seen it. But Libby and Jill took their time going over and over it. She thought the others were going to wear out that valentine they looked at it so much!

It was Tammy's turn. Apprehensively, she stepped to the closet and retrieved Itty-Bitty from the pocket where she had placed him just before her guests arrived. He looked so little and ordinary. Looking at him made Tammy feel nervous about his flying. Maybe he couldn't do it again. Maybe she had imagined he had done it the first time.

Just as she knew they would, the other girls "ooed" and "aahed" at Itty-Bitty, begging to hold him. Well, at least Linda and Libby did. Jill backed away from the mouse. She was afraid of him. Tammy was afraid Itty-Bitty couldn't fly again. But there was no turning back now.

"This is what makes him fantastic," Tammy said, hopping up with Itty-Bitty in her hand, carrying him to the curio shelf where she shakily lifted him.

She quickly returned to her place in the circle on the floor, waiting like the others for something to happen.

"Why did you put Itty-Bitty over there?" Libby asked.

"Just wait," Tammy hushed her.

They waited another few minutes, but nothing happened.

"What are we waiting for?" Linda asked.

"Just hold your horses," Tammy said, waving her antsy friends back down to sit quietly on the carpet.

Still nothing happened.

"Is he supposed to do something?" Linda asked.

Tammy nodded. What could be wrong with Itty-Bitty? Why wouldn't he fly?

# 11

"Why don't you tell us what's supposed to happen?" Linda asked.

"Because you wouldn't believe it unless you saw it," Tammy explained.

"I know. Itty-Bitty is supposed to jump off the shelf. Is that it?" Jill guessed.

Tammy shook her head. But she couldn't tell her friends what was supposed to happen, that Itty-Bitty could fly. Because they wouldn't believe it. And then they would think she had made the whole thing up. They would think she was a liar like Marcella Starbuckle!

"Well, guess you'll just have to show us your fantastic thing at the next meeting," Libby said, standing up. "That was the rule we decided on. Whoever doesn't have something fantastic can wait till the next time we meet."

"But that means I'm not joined yet!" Tammy

wailed. "And it was my idea to have this club in the first place!"

"You can get joined next time," Jill said, trying to comfort her.

"Well, you can bet that my fantastic thing will be a lot greater than playing a baby song through braces."

" 'Row, Row, Row Your Boat' is not a baby song," Libby defended Jill. "And we agreed that Jill playing a song on her braces was a fantastic thing. You're just angry because your fantastic thing didn't work out. Don't take it out on Jill."

"Well, you're just defending her because of your story about the secret compartment in the Spencer mansion. How do we know there really is a secret compartment in the Spencer mansion?"

"Because Libby said so," Linda said. "Libby never lies."

"All right, then," Tammy said, eyeing her friends with a haughty look. "I'm saying that my mouse, Itty-Bitty, can fly. So now you have to believe me."

"He can fly?" Jill asked with surprise. "Was that what you were trying to show us?"

Tammy nodded her head. "So now I get joined in the club, too. If you believe Libby, you have to believe me."

"But your mouse wouldn't fly," Jill said.

"He did yesterday," Tammy defended herself.

"But he didn't today," Linda said.

"But I'm telling you he did. Just like Libby told us about the secret compartment. She didn't have to prove anything."

"Okay, then," Linda said, taking charge. "Libby and Tammy will be disqualified from the club until the next meeting. Then they can either prove for sure the fantastic things they said or bring something new that is fantastic. Everybody agreed?"

They all nodded.

"I know what you could do that would be fantastic!" Jill yelled. "And you could both do it together!"

"What?" Libby and Tammy asked at the same time.

"You could find out who stole the school valentines."

"That's a great idea," Linda agreed.

"No, it's not," Tammy argued. "That might take forever! We want to get joined earlier than that." And, of course, Tammy didn't want anyone to know that *she* had taken the valentines.

Libby smiled. "Besides, I bet those valentines are going to show up at school soon."

Tammy eyed Libby — did she suspect that

Tammy was the one who stole the valentines? Was she guessing that Tammy would return them to school so Jill and Linda would quit suggesting that she and Tammy hunt for them? She was right — Tammy would return them!

"We can meet at my Grandma and Grandpa's house tomorrow," Linda offered. Linda lived with her grandparents while her mom and dad traveled and performed their magic act from city to city all over the country.

"But not until after basketball practice," Libby, Jill and Tammy said in unison, all rolling their eyes.

After her friends left, Tammy scooped Itty-Bitty out of her pocket and gave him a talk.

"Why didn't you fly today? Don't you realize what you've done to me? You made me look silly! Couldn't you just fly and get me joined to the club? I'm not sure I love you anymore."

Then she put Itty-Bitty in the closet and went to find Meredith. If anybody could think of something fantastic that Tammy could use to impress her friends, it would be Meredith. Her room was a treasure-trove of weird stuff.

"What are you doing?" she asked her sister.

Meredith was leaning over her work table again, fitting the plastic mold she had made onto the top of a coffee can, which had been wired from the bottom with two lights that lit up whenever Meredith flipped a switch.

"I am really busy right now," Meredith warned her. "I thought you had company anyway."

"They left."

"Well, why don't you go talk to Mom?"

"Because I want to talk to you. I want to know if you have any neat experiments I could borrow."

Meredith stopped and looked at Tammy. "Since when did you get interested in science?"

Tammy shrugged. "Since I need something to show my friends that would make me fantastic."

Meredith grinned. "And you think *my* science projects could do that for you? You? Who calls me Einstein and Weird Meredith and Pain Brain?"

Tammy glanced down. "Maybe I was wrong about all those things."

Meredith said, "You mean that now that you need my help, you've changed your mind. You know what your trouble is, Tammy? You aren't loyal to anything or anybody."

"I am, too. I still eat ant sandwiches. That's being loyal to Dad."

"That is not being loyal to Dad. Being loyal to Dad would be if you loved him no matter whether he left or not."

"Why should I? He doesn't love me."

"Do you always have to have somebody love you first?"

"Oh, what do *you* know about it, Einstein?" Tammy grumbled, sauntering away from Meredith.

"See what I mean?" Meredith called after her.

Tammy found her mother in the garage, changing the oil on the car. "Know anything fantastic about me?" she asked.

"Well, let's see," Mrs. Collins began. "You're my daughter. That's pretty fantastic."

"Mom," Tammy moaned. "Get serious."

Mrs. Collins stood up from where she had been leaning over the car engine, holding a can of oil. "There must be something pretty fantastic about you. One of your friends came to see me at work this afternoon."

"Who! Why!"

"I can't tell," Mrs. Collins said. "It's a secret. I gave my word not to tell."

"But why would someone go to see you at work?"

Her mother smiled. "I *can* tell you that it has something to do with school valentines."

Tammy's heart sank. "Did this person question you about school valentines?"

Her mom nodded.

"But you don't know anything about school valentines, do you?"

"I tried to help," her mother said.

Oh, no, Tammy thought — she had underestimated Libby Grimes. She never thought that Libby would go talk to her mother about the school valentines!

"But can't you tell me anything?"

Her mother hesitated. "All I can say is that you must be a very special person for your friend to go to the trouble to talk to me about you."

Tammy didn't feel special. She felt trapped! She was about to be found out as the valentine thief! Well, she would show that Libby Grimes.

She marched back to her room and flung open the door to her closet. She dug out every last school valentine from Itty-Bitty's box. She was going to take them back to school. She was sorry she had taken them in the first place. But then she noticed something. The valentines were all right, but the envelopes that contained them were ragged and chewed where Itty-Bitty had nested in them. She couldn't take the valentines back to school looking like that!

She pulled each valentine out of its envelope, stacking them into a pile to take back to school.

Then she threw away all of the envelopes into the trash. Tomorrow she would take the valentines back and divide them up equally among the twenty-five valentine boxes in her classroom. Since there were a hundred and fifty valentines, each person would get six valentines. That was a lot better than some people getting twice that many and others getting half or none. She was proud of herself for thinking of such a good idea.

Then something suddenly occurred to her. Where was Itty-Bitty? She hadn't seen him at all since placing him in the closet when she had been so angry with him.

He was lost. Well, maybe he had gotten tired of her, just like her father. Maybe he decided to leave, to find a nicer place to be. Maybe he had decided to fly after all, and flew away, never to return again. She hoped not. Maybe he left when she took his valentines away. She retrieved some old newspaper from downstairs and shredded it up to make him a new bed, hoping he would come back to chew on it.

She looked for him again after supper, thinking he might have found the new newspaper bed she had fixed for him. But he wasn't there. She finally gave up and went to bed. Maybe she fell asleep. She didn't know. But something woke her in the night. Something warm and fuzzy against her cheek.

It was Itty-Bitty. He nuzzled against her face on the pillow. He peeped. Tammy reached out and curled her hand around him. Then she mumbled sleepily to him, "I love you, Itty-Bitty. Whether you can fly or not."

# 12

The next morning, Tammy stashed the school valentines in her book bag and raced off to school. She wanted to be early so she could return them to the empty boxes before anyone else came.

Unfortunately, Marcella Starbuckle saw Tammy running and called out to her, "Hey, Tammy, what's your big hurry?"

Oh, boy, Tammy thought. This was just what she didn't need — Marcella slowing her down. So she thought of a way to get rid of Marcella and to disguise herself at the same time. "Hello, Earthling," she said to Marcella in a low, monotone voice. "Is my disguise really that good? Do I look like someone you know?"

Marcella looked at Tammy with a puzzled expression. "You look like Tammy. But you don't sound like Tammy. Tammy's voice always sounds louder. And she usually makes faces at me."

Tammy gulped. She *did* always make faces at Marcella. She felt ashamed that she had treated Marcella that way, and she wished she didn't have to lie to Marcella right now, but it was the only way.

"I'm not Tammy," Tammy called to Marcella. "I'm an alien from outer space that made myself look like Tammy."

Marcella believed Tammy! She ran after her yelling, "Can I see your spaceship? Please? I won't touch anything."

"Sorry," Tammy said. "My spaceship is parked too far from here to let you look at it."

"Well, why didn't you park it closer to the school?"

Tammy shrugged. Then she thought of something. "I didn't want to scare anyone. Especially Tammy. I can't let her see me. I can't let her know I've disguised myself to look exactly like her."

Marcella nodded with understanding. "But what are you going to do when she shows up for school? When there are two of you?"

"I'll leave before that happens," Tammy assured her. "But I could use some help. Want to be my lookout? Watch for Tammy so I can disappear when she shows up?"

Marcella nodded. "Sure. I can do that. I can wait outside the school building and watch for her."

Then she looked confused. "But what are you going to do inside the school?"

Tammy rubbed her chin with thought. Then she decided on something. "I'm going inside the school to collect samples."

"Samples of what?" Marcella asked.

"Samples of homework and textbooks and things Earth children use. But don't worry. I'll bring them back. I'll take them to my spaceship and copy them and bring them back."

"Wow," Marcella said. "I wish I could go with you. To make the copies. I wish I could go with you back to your planet. What's the name of your planet, anyway?"

Tammy was losing time by standing out in front of the school talking to Marcella. Impatiently she muttered, "You wouldn't know it. It's in another galaxy." Then she dashed inside the school and scampered quickly to her classroom.

She peeked around the open door to see if anyone was in the room. Mrs. Crandall was sitting at her desk. What was Tammy going to do to get Mrs. Crandall out of the classroom so she could stuff the valentine boxes with valentines?

She had an idea that just might work. She hid her book bag in the girls' bathroom. Except for her English book, which she took with her. Then she walked back out into the hall and out the side doors at the end of the hall near the fourth-grade room. Then she strolled nonchalantly around the side of the school so that Marcella would see her.

Just as she thought: Marcella's eyes bugged out and she dashed inside the school to warn Tammy's made-up alien that the real Tammy was coming.

Tammy sneaked back inside the school to the girls' bathroom again and clamped a hand to her mouth to keep from laughing so hard she might give away her hiding place.

"Here she comes! Here she comes!" Marcella yelled from all the way down the hall. As Tammy suspected, Marcella's outburst alarmed Mrs. Crandall, and she left her classroom to go see what was the matter with Marcella.

The minute Mrs. Crandall left the classroom, Tammy dashed across the hall from the bathroom to the classroom. Then like Santa Claus, she began pulling out stacks of valentines from her bag and filling the boxes with them.

All the while she could hear Mrs. Crandall talking to Marcella down the hall. She wished she had more time to stop and listen to Marcella tell Mrs. Crandall the big fat story of meeting an alien on her walk to school. An alien who looked like Tammy Collins!

Quickly, she stashed her empty bag under her desk and darted out of the room, carrying her English textbook again. Peeking around the hall corner, she could see Mrs. Crandall standing in the hall, facing the other way, talking to Marcella, blocking Marcella's view of the side doors.

Tammy ran for the doors, slipping through them without making a sound. She ran as fast as she could to the front of the school. Then, catching her breath, she strolled slowly through the front doors again.

"There she is," Mrs. Crandall said, catching sight of Tammy. "You're not an alien, are you, Tammy?"

Tammy acted surprised. "An alien?"

"Marcella swears she met someone on the way to school this morning that looked just like you. Someone who was an alien pretending to be you."

"Oh, Marcella," Tammy said, rolling her eyes.

"What's going on? What's going on?" yelled a throng of other classmates as they poured into the school.

Marcella repeated her story of the alien for the rest of the class. Groans and guffaws erupted when she finished telling her story.

"All right, class. The bell will ring soon. Let's move on to our room," Mrs. Crandall said, breaking them up.

Everyone moved toward the classroom. Tammy bounced to her seat, shoving her English book into her desk.

"Mrs. Crandall, the valentines are back!" Libby Grimes shouted from the back of the room.

Everyone stopped what they were doing and ran to their boxes. Tammy ran, too, although with not as much enthusiasm. Mrs. Crandall inspected the boxes. She smiled. "Isn't this wonderful? Whoever took them brought them back. I'm so glad."

"It was the alien who brought them back," Marcella said. "This proves I *did* talk to an alien this morning."

"Ha!" Eddie Wilcox snorted. "This proves that you made up that big story about an alien so nobody would suspect that *you* were the valentine thief!"

Marcella's beaming face clouded. "I am not the valentine thief. Mrs. Crandall can tell you that I'm not. I didn't come anywhere near this room this morning, did I, Mrs. Crandall?"

"Marcella's right, Eddie," Mrs. Crandall said. "She is not the valentine thief. But let's not waste time worrying about how the valentines were returned. Let's just be glad that we have them back."

Mrs. Crandall looked straight at Tammy after she said that. She smiled. Tammy glanced down and quickly shuffled back to her seat. She thought that would be the end of the valentine mystery, but she was wrong.

At recess, Jill bounced over to Tammy and said, "We're going to join Libby into the club. She predicted the valentines would be back at school and now they are. That's fantastic enough to join her."

"No, it's not," Tammy argued. "Anybody could have said the valentines were coming back. It was a coincidence."

"We think it was a prediction," Linda said. "And since Jill and I are the only official members so far, we're the only ones who can vote."

"You can't do that!" Tammy wailed.

"Yes, they can," Libby said. "But it doesn't matter, anyway. Because you have something fantastic that will join you, too."

"What?"

"That alien thing that Marcella was talking about. An alien made itself look like you. Now it's pretty fantastic that that alien picked you to look like. Right?"

Tammy didn't know what to say. She thought that once she brought back the valentines, nobody would talk about them anymore, that everybody would forget about them. But Libby wouldn't quit. And Libby wasn't the only one. Everybody on the playground was talking about them, arguing about whether the alien story was true or not, speculating as to why the valentines had been returned with no envelopes.

"The alien took the envelopes so it can know our names and disguise itself like each and every one of us," Eddie Wilcox said in a scary voice.

"It took the envelopes so it can forge our handwriting," Ryan Soetart said.

Tammy looked around at all the frightened faces of her schoolmates. She had to put a stop to all the rumors her alien story had generated.

"There was no alien," Tammy blurted out. "*I* took the valentines. And the reason I couldn't bring them back in their envelopes was that my mouse chewed them up."

Everyone stopped and stared at Tammy. They were surprised by her confession. No one said anything; then Mrs. Crandall spoke.

"I was sure that you would tell the truth, Tammy," she said, nodding her head with approval.

Tammy sighed with relief. It felt good to have the truth known, so she didn't have to pretend anymore. And it felt especially good that Mrs. Crandall had believed in her, had believed she would admit her mistake. Tammy supposed she knew, too, that when she confessed there would be a consequence to pay for what she did wrong. She was right about that.

"You won't be allowed to attend our Valentine's Day party, Tammy," Mrs. Crandall said.

"I know," Tammy said, dropping her head, shuffling back to the classroom alone.

# 13

No one in the class said anything to Tammy about her confession of having stolen the class valentines. But everybody looked at her long and hard. Tammy kept her eyes pointed down the rest of the day. She felt as though she were an animal at the zoo and people kept staring in at her through a cage.

She wondered now if telling about taking the valentines had helped anyone. Herself? Her classmates? She thought that by not speaking to her, no one wanted to have anything to do with her. And if she didn't talk to someone soon about what had happened, she was sure that she would bust!

She ran to Papadakis's bookstore. He was the only one she could talk to who wouldn't punish her when he found out what she had done. Wasn't being banned from the class Valentine's Day party punishment enough? She hoped that he would think that although stealing the valentines had been wrong, that taking them back was right and telling on herself was right, too.

What she wanted to know was whether Papadakis thought that Libby and Jill and Linda would think her confession was a "fantastic" thing? She still wanted to be a member of the Fantastic Four. Did she dare show up at Linda's house for the meeting and depend on her friends to judge what she had done as worthy of being fantastic? Suppose all they could think about was that she had taken the valentines in the first place? That, they could easily argue, was not fantastic.

She told Papadakis all about the school valentines. She told him all about why she took the valentines in the first place. How she wanted more than three measly valentines. How it didn't seem fair that others in her class got more than she did. How she was really sad that she didn't even get a valentine from her father. "But, of course, you know all about me taking them," Tammy said. "Libby Grimes came to see you thinking I might have done it."

"No," Papadakis corrected her. "Libby Grimes came to ask me what kind of school valentine you would like. She drew your name."

Tammy stood there stunned. "Then you didn't know about me taking the school valentines?"

"No," Papadakis said.

"Well, now that you know, what do you think of me? Do you think I am a terrible thief? Are you going to stop being my friend, just like my dad stopped being my father?"

"I don't think you are a terrible thief," Papadakis said. "I think you are my fantastic friend for taking the valentines back. I suspect your papa would think so, too, if he ever knew. And that is what you should tell your friends. They will think you are fantastic for doing that, too."

"No, they won't," Tammy argued. "They'll think I was terrible for taking the valentines in the first place."

"Not if you explain why. How you felt. Your friends are more understanding than you think. That Libby Grimes is, anyway. I don't know any others."

"Libby won't believe me," Tammy said. "She might think I was bringing back the valentines because I was afraid of getting caught. She wouldn't think I was truly sorry that I took them. You see, I wouldn't believe about her seeing a secret compartment in old Mr. Spencer's mansion. That

was the fantastic thing she told at our meeting."
Tammy clapped a hand to her mouth. "Oops! I
wasn't supposed to tell. You won't tell anybody,
will you, Papadakis?"

Papadakis shook his head. "I will not tell." He
winked at her. "What I will do is show you a secret
of my own. I will show you my secret so you can
remember that you must believe in yourself,
whether your friends do or not."

Papadakis motioned for Tammy to stand behind
his wheelchair and hold on to the handles to secure
the chair in one spot. Then he leaned forward and
lifted each of his legs off of the footrests that extended from the bottom of the chair.

"What are you doing, Papadakis?" Tammy
asked, frightened when she saw his feet plop to the
floor with heavy thuds. She didn't like not knowing what he was going to do.

"I am going to show you how to believe," he
repeated. Then he leaned down and folded the
footrests to the sides of his chair so they would be
out of the way.

"Are you going to try to stand up, Papadakis?"
Tammy asked nervously.

Papadakis chuckled. "Let me show you."

He scooted his body to the front edge of the chair
seat. He tottered there a few moments. Tammy

held her breath. Surely he was not going to do what she thought. She didn't want him to do anything dangerous, anything that might hurt him.

Papadakis planted his hands firmly on the arms of his chair and strained with all his might to lift himself up out of the chair. "You were the one who got me thinking," he explained between heavy gasps. "You were the one who gave me the idea that I should try to learn to walk again."

Tammy didn't know what to say. *She* had been the one? But she didn't want to be the one! She didn't want to cause Papadakis any harm. And right now, although she stood behind him and couldn't see his face, she could see the veins on his arms popping out as he strained to lift himself up. She could hear his breathing becoming more and more labored. Part of her wanted him to stop, to ease her fears; another part of her wanted him to do it, to succeed.

Papadakis's upper body shook as he slowly, barely lifted himself off the seat of the chair. His knees wobbled. His arms continued to shake in uncontrollable spasms. But the worst part was the painful groans coming from Papadakis; his rich and gusty voice had been reduced to low, guttural sounds.

He reached a midway point where he was half-standing and half-sitting. Then, like a fortress of blocks Tammy used to build when she was younger, he suddenly collapsed back into the chair. He leaned to one side in agony, gasping and sputtering.

Tammy couldn't say anything. She was awed by his attempt to stand but also felt embarrassed for having witnessed his failure.

"You almost did it," she said, moving out from behind the chair.

Papadakis held his head with his hands. "I did it for all the wrong reasons. I wanted to impress you. All I did was disappoint myself. I can't do it for you. I have to do it for me."

Tammy backed away from Papadakis. "I have to go now. You're all right, aren't you?"

Papadakis still breathed funny, but he lifted an arm and waved at her, not looking her in the eye. "I'm all right. All that is hurt is my pride."

"Well, maybe I'll see you later," she said quickly, dashing out of the store. If she had had doubts about whether she should go to the club meeting, depending on her bringing the valentines back to school to get her joined, she was sure now that her friends would never accept her for doing that.

She understood now why her classmates had kept quiet after she confessed to taking the valentines — they were embarrassed for her. Just like she was embarrassed for Papadakis. No, she would say nothing about the stolen valentines. Only one thing could help get her back into the good graces of her friends: that was if Itty-Bitty would fly for them. She *had* to gamble on it.

She ran home. Itty-Bitty was in the box filled with shredded newspaper in her closet. He was her only hope of bringing something fantastic to the club meeting at Linda's house.

As she ran to Linda's house, she tried to forget all about Papadakis. In fact, she figured she probably wouldn't go back to his bookstore ever again. What did he know about getting joined into a club? He was just an aging man in a wheelchair. She didn't need him.

But then she felt something tug at her. Maybe Papadakis needed *her*.

"I brought a letter today," Libby announced when the four of them were seated in a circle on the floor of Linda's room. "I went to see Mr. Spencer after school. I'm really glad I did, too, because it made him happy to have somebody to talk to."

Linda asked, "What does the letter say?"

Jill read the letter. "It says that Mr. Spencer does have a secret compartment in his parlor. And it says that nobody but him and Libby Grimes knows

where the lever is that opens the secret compartment."

"That's neat," Linda gasped.

"Fantastic even," Jill agreed.

"So I'm in the club?" Libby asked.

Linda nodded and Jill nodded. That meant that
Libby was officially joined.

Tammy sat on her heels and sulked. What was
so fantastic about a dumb old secret compartment,
anyway? Especially since the rest of them didn't get
to look at it and know how to open it themselves.
But she didn't say one word, since Libby and the
others were good enough not to mention all the
trouble she had had at school that day.

"Your turn, Tammy," Linda said.

Tammy scooped Itty-Bitty out of her pocket. "I
brought Itty-Bitty with me."

"Are you going to try to get him to fly again?"
Jill asked in a bored tone. "You tried that before."

"It's okay," Libby said. "I told about the secret
compartment before, too. We agreed that Tammy
would have another chance for Itty-Bitty to fly."

"Okay, then, let's see him," Linda said.

Tammy stroked Itty-Bitty's head. The mouse
wriggled between her hands. He was nervous
about something. He wasn't acting like himself at
all.

But she'd try, anyway. She looked around the room for a high shelf where she could set the mouse to give him a place from which to fly.

That's when she spotted Mississippi. Linda's gray cat was crouched under a highboy dresser, gleaming at Itty-Bitty. His yellow eyes stared intently at the mouse. His whole body stiffened, ready to pounce.

Tammy opened her mouth to tell Linda that Mississippi would have to leave the room. Suddenly Itty-Bitty wriggled free, popping out from between her folded palms. He skittered straight for the bed. But Mississippi snatched him between his teeth before Itty-Bitty could disappear.

Tammy shrieked, "He's got Itty-Bitty! Do something! He's going to kill him!"

Linda jumped up and grabbed Mississippi. She wrenched Itty-Bitty out of Mississippi's mouth. Itty-Bitty had flapped around like a beached fish in Mississippi's mouth, peeping loudly and continuously. But when Linda released him, he lay still in her hand, a trail of blood staining the snow white fur at his neck.

Linda handed Itty-Bitty to Tammy. "Oh, Tammy, I'm so sorry. Mississippi didn't mean to do something bad. He didn't understand that Itty-Bitty was not supposed to be caught."

"He isn't dead, is he?" Jill asked.

"Maybe he'll be all right. If you get him to an animal doctor," Libby said.

Tammy carefully tucked Itty-Bitty into her pocket. Then she dashed out of Linda's house. There was only one person in the world who could help her save her tiny friend, only one person who could change bad things into good. Papadakis.

# 14

Tammy ran as fast as she could to Papadakis's bookstore. She couldn't run home and call her mom at work or tell Meredith about Itty-Bitty. They wouldn't understand. And although she had been to Dr. Ohman, the veterinarian, when her dog Buttons got shots and things, she was scared to go there by herself.

But when she entered the store, she couldn't *find* Papadakis to tell him. His familiar baritone voice wasn't singing out. She listened carefully for the *tick, tick, tick* of his wheelchair. The store was eerily quiet.

She yelled out his name and then listened for a response. Nothing. Had Papadakis gone somewhere? But he wouldn't leave the store unlocked if he had. And although it was almost five o'clock, closing time, he wouldn't have forgotten to turn the sign on the door to let people know that he was closed.

"Papadakis!" Tammy yelled again. "Papadakis! Where are you?"

Then Tammy heard it: a low, muffled sound at the back of the store. She ran quickly to where it came from. She found Papadakis lying on the floor in front of his wheelchair. His eyes were open and he was breathing fine, but Tammy was frightened to see him sprawled on the floor like that. She didn't know what to do.

"Tammy, I did it!" Papadakis said, looking up at her. "I stood up and walked two steps!"

"But you're on the floor," Tammy said, her usual strong voice now weak and apprehensive.

"Oh, this," Papadakis said, laughing. "Well, yes, I fell flat on my face. Right after I walked the two steps. But I did walk those two steps. You believe me, don't you?"

Tammy couldn't think about believing or not believing. She was worried about how Papadakis was going to get back into his chair. She was worried about Itty-Bitty dying! She couldn't even think about whether she believed Papadakis had walked.

"Oh, Papadakis, something terrible has hap-

pened!" Tammy cried. "It's Itty-Bitty. He was attacked by a cat!"

Tammy eased Itty-Bitty out of her pocket and
held him out for Papadakis to see, crouching on the
floor next to him. The mouse lay on his side on
Tammy's hand. His tiny chest moved, but otherwise he was still.

It was so strange talking to Papadakis that way:
he lay on the floor, actually smiling up at her, while
she stood above him fretting over Itty-Bitty. "You
must take him down the street to Doc Ohman,"
Papadakis said. "Take some money from the cash
register. You can pay me back later."

"But Papadakis," Tammy wailed. "I can't leave
*you*. I have to help you get back in your chair.
Suppose a customer came in?"

"Take the key out of the register, too," Papadakis said. "Lock the front door on your way
out. Then you can come back after seeing
Doc Ohman. Go on! Hurry! Before Doc Ohman
goes home for the day. Before Itty-Bitty gets
worse!"

"But what if something happens to you!"
Tammy whimpered. "What if you're really hurt
only you don't know it?"

"Don't you believe me when I say that I

walked?" Papadakis questioned her. "Don't you believe me when I say that I'm all right?"

"But you look so helpless down there on the floor," Tammy said. "I would feel better if you were in your chair."

"Not me," Papadakis said, again smiling up at her. "I feel better down here than I've felt in a long time. I walked, Tammy! I walked! Now go on. Go get the key and some money from the register. Go catch Doc Ohman before he leaves his office."

Tammy hesitated. "Are you sure? You want me to take money out of your cash register? How do you know I won't take too much? I'm a thief, you know."

Papadakis inhaled deeply. "Tammy, I believe in you. I know you'll only take as much money as you need. I know that you will pay me back. If I believe in you, why can't you believe in yourself?"

"Because I can't trust myself," Tammy admitted. "I took the class valentines. And I stole Itty-Bitty from Meredith. And I've stolen things from Kreske's store. I don't want to steal from you, too, Papadakis. I don't want to."

"Tammy, you are making me angry," Papadakis yelled up at her from the floor. Then he stopped and waited a moment, his voice returning to normal. "Please do as I say. It was you who gave me the idea to try to walk: You made me believe in myself again. Don't fail me now by not allowing me to keep believing in you. Then I'll lose confidence in myself."

Tammy hesitated. "Only if you promise me that you'll be all right here by yourself."

"Of course I'll be all right. I am Papadakis, the only survivor of two hundred. This is nothing. Lying here on this floor is nothing at all. I am just resting actually — resting so I will have the strength to pull myself up and try walking again."

Tammy ran to the cash register, which sat on a low table in the middle of the store. It had so many buttons on it that she wasn't sure which one to punch to make the drawer slide open. But she had watched clerks work cash registers before. She punched the big button on the right that said "no sale." The register chugged and chinked and opened!

She quickly pulled out two 20-dollar bills and a ring with a key on it that lay in one of the drawer's cubicles. "I've got the money and the key!" she yelled out to Papadakis. "I'm leaving now. I'll be back just as soon as I can."

She dashed to the door and quickly stepped out of it, locking it with the key behind her. She pulled Itty-Bitty out of her pocket to look at him. He was still breathing. She didn't take her eyes off the mouse as she galloped down the sidewalk to Doctor Ohman's office. If he died, she didn't know what she would do. She was just glad that Papadakis didn't say "I told you so" for taking the mouse to the club meeting. Then she would have felt twice as rotten as she already did.

Tammy also felt scared. The Riverview Veterinary Clinic was not a place she liked at all. She remembered how Buttons would whimper and moan whenever he came to the clinic because he knew something painful was going to happen to him. Tammy was afraid that something painful might happen now; she was afraid that Itty-Bitty was going to die. And there would be no one there with her — she was all alone.

"How did it happen?" Doctor Ohman asked, gently taking Itty-Bitty from Tammy.

Tammy explained the whole thing to Doctor Ohman. "That stupid Linda," she said at the end of her story. "She should have known that a cat would attack a mouse. Cats naturally like to chase mice."

Doctor Ohman didn't say a word. That was worse than if he had said, "*You* should have known that, Tammy. But you were only thinking about one thing: getting joined to that club."

Tammy knew that Doctor Ohman wouldn't

really say something like that to her; it was actually a voice inside her that said it. And that same voice made her feel terrible that she had left Papadakis alone back at his store, lying on the floor.

Old gray-headed Dr. Ohman carefully told Tammy, "I don't get many mice in my practice. But I'll try to help your mouse the best I can."

Tammy asked the doctor, "What are you going to do?"

Then she winced when he said, "See how deep the bite is? Sew it up. Disinfect the wound."

Tammy paced around the small waiting room for the longest time, worrying. She worried about Itty-Bitty. Then she worried about Papadakis. They were her two best friends in the world. It was no coincidence that both of them were in trouble, she decided. Bad things happened whenever she was around her friends. Jill's valentine paper got ruined in the mud puddle. Itty-Bitty got hurt by Mississippi. Papadakis fell on the floor. And her father had to leave Riverview altogether. She was convinced that she was a jinx!

Finally Doctor Ohman came out, holding Itty-Bitty in the palm of his hand. "Your mouse is feeling much better. I think he was more stunned than hurt." He handed Itty-Bitty to Tammy. "Just give him a lot of love. He should be better soon."

Tammy thanked Doctor Ohman and gave him Papadakis's money. She felt a whole lot better. In fact, she even smiled. She had done it! She had helped Itty-Bitty. She carefully ran with Itty-Bitty in her palm back to the bookstore to tell Papadakis the good news. She quickly unlocked the door and ran to where he lay on the floor.

"Papadakis! Papadakis! Guess what! Itty-Bitty is going to be all right!"

Papadakis groaned from the floor. He wasn't smiling now. In fact, his eyes were closed and his face was twisted with pain.

"What happened?" Tammy asked with alarm.

"I tried to get back into my chair," Papadakis mumbled. "I hit my head hard when I fell back down," he explained. Then he said some more words that Tammy couldn't understand, because he seemed to be falling asleep when he said them.

Tammy knew that Papadakis needed help — more help than she could give him. She wished someone else were around to help him, but she was the only one. Yet she had helped Itty-Bitty. She took him to Doctor Ohman all by herself. Somehow she had to get help for Papadakis the same way.

Without thinking whether she could do it or not, Tammy ran to the phone near the cash register and picked up the receiver. She called her mother at the hospital. Her mother was a nurse. She would know what to do.

Not long after that, Tammy's mom arrived in an ambulance with two men. The men lifted Papadakis onto a rolling bed and took him away to the hospital.

"You were a brave girl for helping that man the way you did," Tammy's mom said, hugging Tammy to her.

Any other time Tammy might have enjoyed being a hero, but she knew that it was her fault that Papadakis got hurt in the first place. Her and her big ideas for him to walk. From then on, Tammy vowed, she was going to stay away from her friends. She didn't want them getting hurt because of her.

# 15

The next day, Tammy pretended to be sick and stayed home from school. She suspected that she hadn't really fooled her mother, though. Her mother didn't even take her temperature. Tammy's mother seemed to sense that Tammy had sad feelings rather than actually being sick.

"Your friend, Mr. Papadakis, is going to be fine," her mother told her. "I called the hospital to check on him. He only had a slight concussion, a bump on the head. He'll be leaving the hospital today."

Tammy knew that her mom told her all of that to make her feel better, and she did feel relieved that Papadakis was going to be all right. But she was not going to visit him ever again. She didn't want any more bad things to happen to him.

Later that afternoon, Meredith called through Tammy's bedroom door, "Tammy, there's somebody here to see you."

"Who is it?" Tammy asked.

"It's Linda Cappanelli," Meredith said.

"Tell her I don't want to talk to her. Tell her to go away!"

Meredith said one last thing. "I'm not your answering service, you know?"

Tammy didn't care what Meredith was; she was not going to talk to Linda. Linda was probably here to say how sorry she was about Itty-Bitty getting hurt by her cat. Well, that was fine, but Tammy was afraid she might cause something bad to happen to Linda the way she had caused Itty-Bitty to get hurt and Papadakis to bump his head. She felt scared and worried and angry all at the same time.

All day Itty-Bitty lay flat on Tammy's pillow. When she had taken him home the day before, she made a dent in the pillow with her fist and lay Itty-Bitty there. He seemed to be sleeping. But Tammy was still scared that he might be dying. If Itty-Bitty died, it would be all her fault.

Tammy lay her head on the pillow next to Itty-Bitty. She stroked the tiny form next to her. She wondered if this was the way her mother felt when she was sick. Did she feel awful? Like she would rather be the sick person herself than watch someone she loved feel so miserable?

She wondered if her father had ever felt that

way. Meredith used to tell a story about when she and their parents brought Tammy home from the hospital. Tammy never believed Meredith because she would only have been three years old at the time, but the story made her feel good when she thought about it. It was the story about how her father almost drove off the side of the road from looking at the newborn Tammy.

How could anybody who had felt so much love for someone leave them behind? Not call? Not send a valentine? Maybe only cute babies could cause a parent to pay attention, Tammy supposed.

Itty-Bitty stirred on the pillow next to her. He twisted himself upright, sitting stretched out on his legs. He peeped. Tammy stroked his back. Itty-Bitty was coming around! He was getting better!

Tammy was filled with joy — she was so happy that she made a promise to herself that she would never let Itty-Bitty be in such a dangerous situation again. Ever!

She fed him some lettuce and tiny bits of cheese. It was like watching him eat for the first time. She waited as he rolled the bit of cheese between his front paws, gnawing on it, crumbs falling around him. His little mouth vibrated with his chewing. Tammy thought this simple act was about the best thing to see in the world!

Somehow, she had to think of a better way to protect Itty-Bitty. She couldn't let him run loose anymore; he might get lost. Or Tammy's dog, Buttons, might run into her room, find the mouse and do the same thing that Mississippi had done. No, Tammy would need to fix Itty-Bitty a cage, to keep him safe. It was for his own good.

What about the cage that Meredith had brought Itty-Bitty home in? What had happened to it?

Tammy had to find it. Even if it meant risking that Meredith would discover she had taken Itty-Bitty. But Tammy could always say that she had suddenly found Itty-Bitty, and Meredith might not want Itty-Bitty back now anyway — she had her planarian worms. What would she want with a mouse now?

Then Tammy thought of something else: Even if she managed to get a cage for Itty-Bitty, it was no guarantee that he would be safe. He would still be around *her*, a jinx. She had to do something to make him the safest he could be: She had to give him up. But who would want him as much as she did? Who would love him as much? No one could love him as much as she did. But Meredith might take him back. Meredith would at least care for Itty-Bitty as well as anybody besides Tammy could. And Tammy could check on Itty-Bitty every day if

Meredith had him. She could make sure he had plenty of food and water and that his cage was kept clean.

But would Meredith play with Itty-Bitty? Would she have time to spare from all of her science experiments? And would she still want to use Itty-Bitty to run him through a maze?

Tammy had to risk those possibilities, for Itty-Bitty's sake. Besides, she told herself, if she gave the mouse back to Meredith, she wouldn't have to feel badly anymore that she had stolen him from her sister.

Tammy left Itty-Bitty still eating his lettuce on her pillow. She had to find that cage. She wouldn't be able to sleep or eat herself until she knew that he was safe.

Pulling open the door to her room, she stopped short: something was sitting in the hall just outside her door. It was the cage that Meredith had used to keep Itty-Bitty in that first day. What was it doing here, outside her door? Why had Meredith put it there?

Meredith knew. She knew Tammy had Itty-Bitty. Probably from Linda. But why hadn't she come looking for him? Why instead had she put the cage where Tammy could find it?

Tammy picked up the cage and hurried back

inside her room. Gently, and with reluctance, she placed Itty-Bitty inside the cage. Then she carried the cage across the hall to Meredith's room, sighing with relief that the room was empty, that Meredith was off somewhere, gone on another scientific safari.

She placed the cage on the window seat in Meredith's room so Itty-Bitty could get plenty of sunshine there. She was doing the right thing, she kept telling herself. But she knew that even if she believed that in her mind, she still couldn't convince her heart.

# 16

The next day at school, Linda asked Tammy, "Why wouldn't you talk to me yesterday? I came to your house to say I was sorry."

"I was busy," Tammy said. "Taking care of Itty-Bitty. You know. The Itty-Bitty that your stupid cat attacked."

"My cat is not stupid," Linda said. "All cats attack mice. It's what they do. Just like dogs chase cats."

"Well, you should have known Mississippi would do that. You should have tied him up or something."

Linda glanced down. "I should have put Mississippi in another room while Itty-Bitty was there. But I was so excited about having the meeting at my house that I forgot." She looked up at Tammy. "Everybody decided when you left that we want to join you in the club."

"Why?"

"Because Itty-Bitty is fantastic. And you own him. So you are fantastic."

"But you didn't see him fly," Tammy said. "You're just joining me to the club because you feel bad about Itty-Bitty getting hurt."

Linda didn't argue. "How is he? Is he going to be all right?"

Tammy nodded. "No thanks to your cat."

Linda glanced down again. "Well, are you going to join the club?"

"I don't know," Tammy said, hesitating. She didn't want any more bad things to happen.

"We thought of something else," Linda confided. "Something fantastic you did that could get you joined to the club."

"What?"

"You brought back the school valentines. During our meeting, Libby was the one who said it was a brave thing to do."

"Libby said that?" Tammy asked with surprise. "Why would she say a thing like that?"

Linda smiled. "She said you are a brave person. She found out yesterday from that crippled bookstore owner that you rescued him when he fell out of his wheelchair. She said that proves for sure that you are brave."

Tammy couldn't say anything for a moment. She realized that Linda viewed her actions very differently than how she herself did. Libby thought she was brave? That really meant something if Libby Grimes thought so — Libby was smart, and if she thought something, others would think it, too.

But what good was bringing back the school valentines and rescuing Papadakis — if she had to spend the whole class valentine party in the detention room like Mrs. Crandall said? She would be there alone. What good was bravery then, she asked Linda.

"Well, you'll still get your special valentine. Mrs. Crandall won't take that away from you."

"I don't want a special valentine," Tammy confided. "All I want is for nothing bad to happen anymore. I guess if I'm alone and away from everybody else, nothing can go wrong. Bad things happen when I'm around."

"You don't *really* believe that, do you?" Linda asked wide-eyed.

Tammy said, "I took the valentines, didn't I?" Linda nodded.

"Well, I made Papadakis fall out of his wheelchair, too."

Linda stared at Tammy for a moment. Then she eased away, as if she believed now what Tammy said.

When the last bell of the school day rang, Tammy didn't run to see Papadakis. She walked home slowly. All the way she wondered what he was doing. Was he singing? Was he writing poetry?

She hoped he was not trying to walk. She reasoned that if she didn't visit him again, he wouldn't try walking, since she had given him the idea in the first place. And if he didn't try walking, he wouldn't hurt himself. And if she didn't take him the money that she owed him for Itty-Bitty to get treated by Doctor Ohman, then he would stop believing in her — he would think she was a thief for sure. Then he would stop trying to walk.

She trudged into her house and up the stairs to her room. Meredith was waiting for her in the hallway. "You had my mouse all along," she stated, eyeing Tammy.

"Yeah, it was me who took him," Tammy admitted.

"But why did you bring him back to me?" Meredith asked.

"Because he belongs to you," Tammy said.

"Maybe once. But not anymore," Meredith told her. "And you just didn't suddenly start feeling guilty about taking him from me."

"I thought he would be safer with you," Tammy explained.

"You changed your mind about being an animal-rights believer?"

"No," Tammy said. "I found out I am a jinx, and I didn't want anything to happen to Itty-Bitty because of it. He's already been attacked by Linda's cat. I didn't want anything else to happen to him."

Meredith rolled her eyes and sniffed. "A jinx! That's the most unscientific thing I've ever heard of. Nobody's a jinx. That's superstition."

Tammy was glad to hear Meredith say that. She wanted to believe that she wasn't a jinx, and it helped to hear Meredith say it, though she still had doubts. "You might think so," Tammy said, "but I'm the one who's seen it happen. All kinds of bad things keep happening to me. That's why I want you to have Itty-Bitty back. So he won't get hurt."

"How could he get hurt?" Meredith asked.

"Itty-Bitty can fly," Tammy said in a secretive voice.

"Oh, Tammy," Meredith said, rolling her eyes. "Mice can't fly."

"Itty-Bitty can."

"How?"

"I don't know how," Tammy admitted, "but I think it's because I believe that he can. Which makes him believe that he can. He wouldn't fly when I tried to show Libby and Linda and Jill. But that was because I wanted him to fly so I could get joined to a club. Not because I believed he could do it."

Meredith cast Tammy a strange look. "Maybe I *should* be the one to take care of him. Next thing you're going to tell me is that he can open his cage door."

"Well, he could, if somebody believed he could do it enough to make him believe it, too," Tammy cried.

"Ha!" Meredith snorted. "The next thing you're going to tell me is that the mouse can write poetry. I could believe your story about you being a jinx before I'd believe a mouse could fly or open his cage. But the fact is, I don't believe any of it. I believe you ought to take him back to prove to yourself all of it isn't true."

Tammy wouldn't follow Meredith into her room. She wouldn't take Itty-Bitty back, even though she wanted to more than anything. Because if she took him back, she still believed that something bad would happen, and she just couldn't stand for that. She wanted only good things for Itty-Bitty.

She went back to her room and wrote a poem to Itty-Bitty. Writing a poem couldn't cause him any harm, she decided. When she was finished, she slipped it under Meredith's bedroom door. She titled it "Valentine to a Flying Mouse," so Meredith would know who it was for. It read:

I love Itty-Bitty
Enough to believe
He is free
To be whatever he wants to be
Unconditionally.

# 17

At school the next day, Libby tugged on Tammy's blouse at the water fountain.

"How come you haven't been to see Papadakis? He wonders why you haven't been back."

Tammy shrugged her shoulders and walked away, but Libby didn't give up easily. She followed Tammy. "Don't you want to know how he's doing? Don't you care about him anymore?"

"How's he doing?" Tammy asked. She said it in a very offhanded way so as not to show much interest. She didn't want Libby to tell Papadakis that she still cared about him — Papadakis would be better off thinking Tammy was no longer his friend. She didn't want to give him any more ideas about walking.

"He can stand up all by himself. You should see him, Tammy," Libby said, her eyes lighting up. "It's really something."

Tammy frowned. "Well, it won't be something if he falls down again."

"Is that what you're afraid of?" Libby asked. "If Papadakis isn't afraid, why are you?"

Tammy glanced down. "I just don't want him to hurt himself. That's all."

Libby nodded. "I know. I've worried about that, too. What he needs is something to help him stand and walk so he won't fall down."

"A walker," Tammy said. "You know. One of those metal-cage-things that older people use to get around."

"That's exactly it!" Libby squealed. "Where can we get one?"

Tammy thought for a moment. "My dad could get one."

"How?"

Tammy said, "He sells them to hospitals and to people that need them. That's what he does. He works for a company that sells those kinds of things."

"Then you could get one?" Libby asked hopefully.

"I don't know," Tammy said thoughtfully. "He lives somewhere else. And we don't talk much," she said, glancing down.

"Hey, maybe that could be a project for our club.

We could raise money to buy a walker for Papadakis," Libby suggested.

"I'm not in the club," Tammy said. "Remember?" She looked away. "Besides, I'm not sure it would be such a good thing for Papadakis to try to walk."

"Why?!"

"Because he might not be able to do it, that's why," Tammy shouted. "Sometimes it's better to leave people alone. The way they are."

Libby cast Tammy a strange look and shuffled away. Tammy wished she could explain what she meant. She wanted to tell Libby about how she had taken Itty-Bitty from Meredith and caused him to get hurt by Linda's cat. Maybe then Libby would understand. Instead, she avoided Libby the rest of the day. But she couldn't stop thinking about Papadakis.

What had she done to him? She had started him thinking about walking, that's what she had done. But now that he thought about it, there was no way that she could get him to quit. He believed that he could do it now. Why couldn't *she* believe it, too? Because things had gone wrong. Papadakis fell. But if there was a way to keep him from falling, maybe Papadakis could walk. That is, if she wasn't around him to jinx him.

Later, at home, she talked to her mother about it. "If you had a friend who wanted to do something with all his heart, but you were afraid he might get hurt, would you help him do it?"

Mrs. Collins glanced up from unloading the dishwasher. "That is a very good question," Mrs. Collins said. "I guess if you love someone enough, you will try to understand that his needs might be different from yours."

Tammy hesitated before asking her next question. But she had to know! "Was that how it was with you and Dad? Did you love him so much that you let him go?"

Mrs. Collins avoided Tammy's questioning look. And, it seemed to Tammy, she avoided the question by changing the subject. "You have been growing up a lot lately. Especially if you can ask a question like that."

"It's true, isn't it?" Tammy asked again. "You let Dad go. Not because you hated him but because you knew he was unhappy. You let him go so he would be happy."

Mrs. Collins said very softly, looking at Tammy with moist eyes, "Yes, Tammy, I let him go. I didn't hold on. Because I knew if he could be free to be happy, maybe he would come back to me."

"But he hasn't!" Tammy exclaimed.

"No, he hasn't," Mrs. Collins sighed. "Still, it was a risk I had to take. When you love somebody, you have to take risks. With love, there are no guarantees."

"Do you still hope he'll come back?" Tammy asked.

Mrs. Collins glanced down. "No. I know now that he's not coming back. But I still think I did the right thing."

Tammy thought about that a moment. She said, "You lost. It was like you gambled and you lost."

Mrs. Collins answered thoughtfully. "I suppose you're right." Then she let the dishwasher door thud shut, and she shrugged. "But are we talking about what happened between me and your father or you and your friend?"

Tammy smiled sheepishly. She had started out talking about Papadakis. But she liked talking about her mom and dad. She liked knowing things her mom could tell her about them. "You mean you would marry Dad all over again? Even if you knew how it was going to turn out? That he was going to leave you?"

Her mother nodded. "It was worth it."

"How? Why?" Tammy didn't understand.

Mrs. Collins cleared her throat. "Because I have you and Meredith and a lot of good memories with your dad."

Tammy sighed. "But wouldn't you be scared to get hurt all over again?"

Mrs. Collins shook her head. Then she looked at Tammy squarely and asked, "Why don't you tell me who the friend is you're talking about? And what you are so afraid of?"

Tammy shrugged. "It's Papadakis. You know. The bookstore owner who fell out of his wheelchair trying to walk?"

"Oh, yes. A delightful man. How's he doing now?"

Tammy looked away. "Okay, I guess. I haven't been to see him."

"Because you're afraid he'll get hurt again?"

Tammy nodded slowly.

Her mother lifted her chin. "You like him a lot, don't you? Well, I wouldn't worry about him if I were you. He's going to do just fine."

"That's what I said," Tammy protested, "but Libby told me that Papadakis is trying to walk again. And he might get hurt. And he needs one of those walker things so he doesn't get hurt. And I think I ought to ask Dad if he could send one to Papadakis. Since he sells them and all. But I'm not sure if I should keep putting the idea to walk into Papadakis's head."

Mrs. Collins looked at Tammy wide-eyed. "That's a lot to have to think about," she finally said.

"Well, what do *you* think?" Tammy asked.

"I think that if Papadakis is determined to walk he will walk whether you do anything to help him or not."

"Yeah. But he might get hurt again," Tammy reminded her.

"Yes. He might do that." She chopped carrots for a while, thinking. Then suddenly she said, "I think you ought to write your father a letter. Explain about Papadakis. See if he can tell you how much a walker would cost. Then you could make more decisions after that." As if to show how much she understood how urgent Tammy felt about solving Papadakis's problem, she offered, "I'll mail your letter express for you. It could get there tomorrow."

Tammy thought her mother's advice sounded good. But then she thought of something. "You think Dad would actually write back to me? I never hear from him."

Her mother frowned. "You would be awfully disappointed if he didn't," she said, as if reminding Tammy there was a great risk that she might never hear from her father. Then her mother smiled. "On the other hand, if he did write back, it would be a great chance for the two of you to do something together."

Tammy smiled. She and her dad could do something together. She wouldn't be alone. That was worth the risk.

# 18

Tammy had just finished writing the letter to her dad that explained all about Papadakis needing a walker. That's when a terrible smell wafted into her room. Meredith was at it again, she supposed. Her sister was cooking up another experiment. Tammy didn't think much about it, except to hold her nose. But then she heard Meredith scream.

Tammy jumped up and ran to Meredith's room. Her sister was at the window near the table where she usually worked on her experiments. The window was wide open, and Meredith was hanging her head out of it, peering down to the ground below.

"What's wrong?" Tammy wanted to know.

Meredith slowly pulled herself back inside, her face white with fear. "Oh, Tammy, something terrible happened. I didn't believe Itty-Bitty could get the cage door open. And I only opened the window to air out my room . . . to get rid of some of the smell."

"He flew out the window," Tammy said slowly. "Itty-Bitty flew."

Meredith nodded. "I didn't believe he would do that. Otherwise, I wouldn't have opened the window."

No! Tammy ran to the window and peered out of it. She couldn't be seeing right. No! It wasn't Itty-Bitty lying on the ground below the window! It wasn't! It wasn't!

Frantically, she ran out of Meredith's room, down the stairs and out the back door. But before she reached him, she stopped short. She inched her way the last few steps to the small ball of white fluff that lay curled in a silent mound.

She stood over him. Finally, she mustered enough courage to bend down and touch him. His eyes were closed. He wasn't breathing. Itty-Bitty was dead.

She collapsed onto the ground beside him. Doubling her knees to her chest, rocking herself to find comfort, she let out one long whimper. And then she could control herself no longer. She sobbed into her knees. She cried and cried.

"Tammy, I'm sorry." It was Meredith.

"Go away," Tammy sputtered.

Meredith walked around her, bending down to examine Itty-Bitty's body. She kneeled next to him, touching him gingerly.

"He's dead," Tammy muttered.

Meredith didn't say anything for a while. She sat next to Tammy and didn't say one word.

"He could fly!" Tammy snapped at Meredith. "Why wouldn't you believe that he could fly?"

Meredith shrugged. "Mice don't ordinarily fly. I thought you were making it up."

Tammy's words softened. "Why didn't I take him back? If I had taken him back, then I would have known not to open any windows. I would have watched out for him."

Meredith shook her head. "You believed you were a jinx. This proves you aren't. Sometimes bad things just happen."

"Papadakis said that, too," Tammy said thoughtfully. "He believed Itty-Bitty could fly, though. Itty-Bitty loved to fly. And he loved me." She burst into tears again.

Meredith stood up. "Come on. I'll help you bury him."

Tammy stood up, too, and watched as her sister lifted Itty-Bitty gently from the ground, carrying him in the palm of her hand.

"You really believe I'm not a jinx?" Tammy

asked. "It wasn't my fault that Itty-Bitty died?"

"Of course it wasn't your fault," Meredith said as they walked to the garage to find the shovel. "It was my fault for not believing you when you tried to warn me." Meredith glanced at her, and for the first time ever, she asked Tammy's opinion about something, as if she believed Tammy would really know better than her. "Where's the best spot to bury Itty-Bitty?" Meredith picked up the shovel from the corner of the garage and waited for Tammy to answer.

"In the flower bed," Tammy mumbled. "Itty-Bitty liked poems I wrote to him with flowers in them. But we can't bury him just like that. He needs a coffin."

Meredith didn't argue. "There's a big matchbox in my room," Meredith offered. "I keep — " She stopped after glancing at Tammy. "I'll go get it." She lay Itty-Bitty down in the flower bed, the shovel next to him, and disappeared inside the house. Soon she returned with the matchbox.

As if understanding that Tammy was too upset to do anything, she placed Itty-Bitty in the matchbox and slid on the cover. Then she dug a small hole and placed the box in it. "Would you like to say a few words?" she asked Tammy.

"I don't know what to say," Tammy mumbled.

"I'll say something." Meredith cleared her throat. "Itty-Bitty was a good mouse. Tammy loved him. And he loved Tammy. He will be remembered."

"Aren't you going to say anything about him flying?" Tammy asked.

Meredith cleared her throat again. "Itty-Bitty was the only mouse in the world that could fly. And he could open his cage gate all by himself. And he was the one who proved to Tammy that she wasn't a jinx. Because what happened to him happened while I was taking care of him. And . . . and it was an accident."

Then she shoveled the small pile of dirt onto the matchbox and covered it up, patting the top with the tip of the shovel.

"He needs a headstone," Tammy said.

Meredith looked around, searching for something that might work for a headstone. A plastic whirligig spun in the air at the edge of the flower bed. Meredith pulled it up from where it was planted and repositioned it at the head of Itty-Bitty's grave.

Tammy smiled when she saw the whirligig twirl in the wind. It was the perfect headstone for a flying mouse.

# 19

Mrs. Crandall stood in front of the class the next day and said, "Raise your hand if you have your homemade valentine ready for tomorrow."

Everyone in the whole class raised their hands except Tammy and Libby Grimes.

"Will you girls have your valentines ready by tomorrow?" Mrs. Crandall asked them.

Libby glanced down. "I'm not sure." She glanced back up. "My valentine is very unusual. It's not written down on paper." She looked at Tammy. "My valentine depends on other people."

Although Tammy was curious as to what Libby meant, since she knew Libby's valentine was meant for her, she said, "It doesn't matter if you don't have one for me, anyway. I won't be at the party to get a valentine. I'll be in the detention room. Right, Mrs. Crandall?"

Mrs. Crandall nodded. "I'm afraid so, Tammy.

But I hope you've learned your lesson about not taking things that don't belong to you. And one way you can show that is by bringing a valentine for the person whose name you drew. Do you have your valentine ready?"

Tammy shrugged. "I'm going to work on it after school."

Mrs. Crandall smiled, content that the two of them would have the valentines ready for the party the next day.

But Tammy noticed that Libby seemed suddenly nervous. She kept looking at Tammy. She kept trying to get Tammy's attention to talk to her. Tammy avoided Libby's searching looks.

What if Libby asked Tammy about Itty-Bitty? Tammy didn't want to talk about Itty-Bitty! She didn't want to tell anyone in the secret club that he was dead. They would always wonder if he could fly. They would always think that Tammy had made it up that Itty-Bitty could fly.

"Are you going to go see Papadakis after school today?" Libby asked Tammy when the last bell rang.

Tammy could avoid her no longer. But she thought it was a little strange that Libby would be asking her *that*, and that she called Papadakis by his name like she knew him well or something.

She shook her head. She was afraid to go see Papadakis. First, because Papadakis had tried to tell her so many things that she hadn't believed: He'd tried to tell her not to use Itty-Bitty to get joined to the secret club. He was right about that. And he had said that she was not a jinx, that bad things that happened, like her father leaving her and Itty-Bitty being hurt by Linda's cat, were not her fault. He was right about that, too.

The second reason she was afraid to go see Papadakis was that he might not believe in *her* anymore. He might believe she was a real thief. After all, she hadn't been to see him to bring him the money that she owed him for Itty-Bitty to get fixed by Doctor Ohman. She didn't know what she would do if Papadakis didn't trust her now; he'd been the only one who believed in her. And if she tried to tell him how Itty-Bitty died, he might not believe that either. He might think it was *her* fault.

If only Tammy had some money to pay Papadakis back. But she didn't. And the only person she could ask was Meredith. But she knew Meredith didn't have any money either. If she asked her mom for money, she would have to tell her all about Itty-Bitty. Tammy wasn't sure she could explain everything so her mother would understand. She was doubly not sure that her mother would ever believe the story about Itty-Bitty.

On the other hand, she sort of wanted to go see Papadakis. She needed him to help her write the valentine for Linda. She was no closer to writing it than when she had asked him to write it two weeks ago, and it had to be finished for the party the next day. What was she going to do?

She walked home slowly, trying to think of something she could write for Linda. But instead of thinking of Linda, she kept thinking about Itty-Bitty. Especially when she pushed her way into her room and he was not there. She missed him something terrible!

Poor Itty-Bitty. If only he could have been a normal mouse, then maybe he would still be alive in his cage. If only he hadn't wanted to fly. But then she realized flying was part of who Itty-Bitty was. Whenever she thought of birds or the wind or the sky itself, she thought of Itty-Bitty.

But, of course, too, when she thought of him, she thought of him dying. Yet even his death wasn't such a bad memory because Meredith had helped her feel better; Meredith was there to help her bury Itty-Bitty. And Meredith had been there to prove to her what Papadakis said: Sometimes bad things just happen.

And Tammy thought about Linda's cat, Mississippi — how he had hurt Itty-Bitty. Mississippi hadn't meant to hurt Itty-Bitty. Tammy could understand that now. It was sort of like Meredith leaving her window open for Itty-Bitty to fly out of. It was an accident.

Tammy took out a piece of paper and pencil and wrote a valentine to Linda Cappanelli:

Roses are red
Violets are blue
I believe what you said
Mississippi didn't mean to be cruel.

P.S. I still believe flowers are good in valentines.
P.S.S. I also believe we could be good friends again.

She drew some hearts with a red marker on the valentine. And then she cut out the paper in the shape of a mouse. A mouse holding a megaphone. For the first time in a long while a warm feeling made Tammy glow with pleasure.

# 20

Tammy waited until the last moment before going out the door to school the next morning to say to her mother, "You don't have to bring valentine treats to the party at school today."

"What do you mean?" her mother wanted to know. "I stayed up half the night making these cookies," she said, pointing to the big heart-shaped cookies with pink cherry icing laid out on wax paper all over the kitchen counter.

"I mean," Tammy said, "I mean I think I may get sick and have to come home. If I'm not at the party, then you don't have to bring anything, right?"

Mrs. Collins quickly stepped towards Tammy and pressed her palm against Tammy's forehead. "You don't feel warm. No temperature. Do you feel sick to your stomach?"

Tammy nodded. It wasn't a lie. She *did* feel sick

to her stomach. Especially at the thought of spending the whole valentine party in the detention room at school.

A quizzical expression came over Mrs. Collins's face. "Is there some reason you don't want to go to the party today, Tammy?" she asked.

"No," Tammy said quickly. But Tammy *did* want to go to the party. The only problem was that she wasn't allowed to go. But if she told her mother that, then she would have to tell her that she had stolen the class valentines, and although she had confessed and brought them back, she could not attend the party.

She didn't really want to go to school, but, of course, she had to, to take Linda the super valentine that she had written. Somehow, though, she had to keep her mom from coming to school so she wouldn't find out about Tammy's bad behavior.

"I can take the cookies to school right now," Tammy offered. "Then you wouldn't have to take off work and come to school later," she suggested to her mother.

"But everything is arranged," her mother insisted. "Besides," she said winking, "I have to bring something besides cookies. I promised Libby Grimes that I would."

"Libby?" Tammy said, confused. "Libby drew

my name to make me a valentine. Is that what your're bringing to school for Libby? My valentine from her?"

Her mother nodded. Then she teased, "And are you going to be surprised!"

Tammy would have stayed to quiz her mother about what kind of valentine Libby had made for her, especially a valentine that required assistance to get it to school, but she had to leave that very moment in order to get to school on time.

Yet when she arrived at school, she wondered if maybe she should have pursued her "sick" condition further, as she had to watch the other valentines be brought to school, many of them secret. She felt left out of the excitement of the plans for the party.

Jill's valentine was so special and huge that her mother had to bring her to school in their car to get the valentine there. Besides that, the valentine was covered with an old sheet. It was the best valentine because everybody kept wanting to know what was under that sheet.

Marcella Starbuckle's valentine was secret, too. She brought it in a big grocery bag. She wouldn't show anyone what was inside the bag, even though Eddie Wilcox tried to tease her into showing it by saying there was nothing in there.

Only Linda would show what she had brought. But she would only show half of it. The outside half. Her valentine was a huge Hershey's Kiss that she'd made out of tin foil. It even had a tissue flag coming out of the top like the real ones. Inside, Linda said, there wasn't a big chocolate drop at all — it was something else. Tammy would never know what. If somebody told her about it after the party, it wouldn't be the same.

Tammy felt sick. She thought about telling Mrs. Crandall so — then maybe she could leave the room and spend the party in the nurse's office and everybody would wonder about her. Only one thing kept her from doing that: She wanted to find out what Libby Grimes had brought for *her*.

Nobody could concentrate on schoolwork all day. And nobody acted like themself. Ryan Soetart didn't make one single smart remark to anybody. Billy Cameron didn't poke anyone with his pencil. Not once! And Eddie Wilcox was uncharacteristically quiet.

Finally, the last hour of the day came. Mrs. Crandall told all of the students in the class to put away their work. The air was charged with excitement. Everyone squirmed in their seats. That's when Mrs. Crandall allowed Tammy to present her valentine to Linda. But after she did, she couldn't wait around to see how Linda liked the valentine. She had to leave the room with a pass to go to the detention room down the hall.

The detention room was a drab little cubicle with a simple table and some chairs around it. Nothing else. No pictures on the walls to look at. No pencil sharpener to grind a pencil in that would break the boredom. No chalkboard to scribble on. Tammy plopped down in one of the chairs and looked up at the ceiling, counting the dots in the tile overhead. That's when she heard the noise filtering from her classroom as her classmates were presenting their valentines to each other. There were cheers and ooh's and aah's.

Tammy lay her head down on the table in front of her and sobbed.

# 21

Tammy heard a noise out in the hall. Someone was coming. She quickly wiped at her eyes with the sleeve of her blouse. She couldn't let anybody know that she had been crying.

The noise *tick, tick, tick*ed and then stopped. Tammy could recognize that noise anywhere. It was the sound of Papadakis's wheelchair!

She jumped out of her seat and pressed her body flat against the wall near the open door of the detention room. She couldn't let Papadakis know that she was only a few feet away from him. She was sure that he had come to school to accuse her of being a thief; he wanted the money back that she had taken from his cash register to pay Doctor Ohman.

But then Tammy heard her mother's voice. Mrs. Collins told Papadakis that he should wait there in the hall for her to go and find Libby Grimes. Now

Tammy understood: Libby had arranged for Tammy's mother to bring Papadakis to school so that Libby's valentine to Tammy would be to get Tammy and Papadakis to be friends again. It was absolutely the worst valentine Tammy could receive!

Now Papadakis could accuse Tammy of being a thief — face to face. And to make matters worse, he could do it in front of Tammy's mother, who would find out that Tammy was in the detention room for stealing school valentines, and would then find out from Papadakis a second reason that she was a thief.

Tammy didn't know what to do. She couldn't run away, because Papadakis would see her dash out of the detention room. Then, besides being in trouble with him and her mother, she would be in double trouble for running away.

The only thing she could think to do was to hide in the detention room closet. But if she passed in front of the open door to get to the closet door, Papadakis would see her. Still, she had to chance it.

Hoping that Papadakis was looking in the other direction, she bent her head low and skittered past the open door. Quickly, she flung open the closet door and slipped inside.

Her palms moistened and her heart throbbed

with fear, especially when she heard the familiar booming voice beckon to her, "Tammy? Is that you, Tammy?"

Then she heard the ticking of the wheelchair as Papadakis rolled closer to the detention room. "Tammy, come out," he called. "I can't come and find you."

She was caught. There was nothing she could do now, she reasoned, except to go out and face Papadakis and try to ease her way past him to run out of the school. She took a deep breath, edged open the closet door, and stepped out into the open doorway.

Papadakis was sitting in the hall in his wheelchair with a large, flat box spread across his lap. Tammy didn't want to look him in the eye. She wanted to skitter past him and run down the hall to the front doors of the school.

But his dancing dark eyes and broad grin held her motionless. "Tammy, my friend, you're as skittish as a mouse," he said. "This isn't like you. Why would you want to hide from your old friend, Papadakis? Why haven't you been to see me?"

Tammy glanced down. "I figured you were here to make me pay back the money I owe you," she stammered. "I don't have the money, Papadakis. I don't even have Itty-Bitty anymore. He died. So even if I ask my mom to pay you the money, she'll never believe me without Itty-Bitty to prove what I say is true."

Papadakis's face clouded. "Tammy, your mother knows all about Itty-Bitty. Your sister told her. And she knows about you not being able to join the others in your class for the party today. Libby told her about that. She understands how you did wrong and set it right . . . how you still have to pay for the wrong. But I am so sorry to hear about Itty-Bitty dying. Doctor Ohman couldn't help him after all, then?"

Tammy shook her head. "It wasn't that. He got okay after the cat attack. You see, I gave him back to my sister, Meredith. So I wouldn't jinx him. And she forgot and left her window open. And, well, Itty-Bitty flew out of it. That's how he died."

Papadakis made a clicking noise in his throat. "No wonder you haven't been to see me. You have been mourning your lost friend. I am doubly surprised and honored that you took the time to write to your father during such a troublesome time."

Tammy's brows jumped. "You know that I wrote a letter to my father?"

Papadakis beamed. "Well, of course! How else could I be part of your valentine from Libby Grimes?"

Tammy scratched her head. "I don't understand."

Papadakis threw up his arms and boomed, "Well, help me with this box and I will show you!"

Tammy held one end of the box while Papadakis pulled and tugged on its contents, sliding a tangle of metal tubing out the other end. The box discarded to one side, Papadakis whirled the folded frame down in front of his chair and quickly pushed and nudged the metal pieces until they blossomed into a square frame with four legs that stretched up to form a box with two handles.

"It's a walker!" Tammy gasped. "My dad sent you the walker!"

Papadakis smiled. "He did indeed. And now I am going to walk for myself." He winked. "As a valentine to you from Libby Grimes. It's not your traditional kind of valentine, mind you, but Libby thought it would be the best valentine you could get."

Tammy nodded. "She was right. Oh, Papadakis, this is wonderful," Tammy said.

"What is wonderful," he said, heaving himself up out of the wheelchair and grasping the walker in front of him, "is that you believed enough in yourself to believe in your father. To write him the letter. And because you believed in each other, it has made me believe, too. I can walk, Tammy."

As if to prove it, he took a big step forward with his left foot and followed it with an equal measure from his right. "I would say," he continued, as he shuffled down the hall with the walker, "that you are pretty wonderful doing this for me. So, you see, my friend, we are even now. I helped you that day with Itty-Bitty, and you have repaid me many times more than money by helping me to walk."

Tammy smiled. She was genuinely thrilled that Papadakis could now learn to walk safely, and she couldn't help but feel a tingle of satisfaction that her dad had done something so heroic at her request.

"Oh, I almost forgot," Papadakis said, sliding his walker into a U-turn and shuffling back to her. When he reached her, he stopped, and balancing himself, he pulled an envelope out of his pocket and handed it to her. "This came enclosed with the walker."

The envelope had Tammy's name scrawled on the outside. Inside were two plane tickets, one in Tammy's name and the other in Meredith's, with Rossville, the town where her father lived, as their destination, dated for the first week in March, during Tammy's spring vacation.

"Oh, Papadakis, does this mean that my father

wants me to come visit him?" She showed the tickets to Papadakis.

He examined the tickets and nodded. "There's nothing written here to explain it, but I sense that your father is a man of actions rather than words. That might seem unusual to a couple of word-smiths such as you and myself. But the message is here, even if it isn't written down." He winked. "This is a valentine, all right."

Tammy smiled and clutched the plane tickets to her chest, as if they were the greatest love poems ever written, which, in her opinion, they were! "You're right, Papadakis. I believe these plane tickets *are* valentines. And I believe you're going to walk some day all by yourself. And I believe I'm going to be a member of the Fantastic Four club."

"So do I," Papadakis said, smiling at her. "So do I."

Tammy beamed. "But before I believe all of that," she said, in a voice much like her old megaphone voice except that it was mellowed by understanding, "I believe in myself. I believe there are a lot of good things about me . . . things I haven't even discovered yet. Things that when I find them out will make me feel like I'm flying."

Papadakis nodded. "I'll walk and you'll fly."

Tammy smiled. "No, Papadakis, we'll both walk

and we'll both fly. And we'll write poetry, too. After all," she said with a wink, "when you believe in yourself, the sky is the limit."

As Papadakis shuffled behind his walker, they walked together down the hall to find Tammy's mom and Libby. But Tammy would swear that her feet were actually floating on air.